MISSION CHAOS

SOS Stories

Edited By Catherine Cook

First published in Great Britain in 2019 by:

Young Writers
Remus House
Coltsfoot Drive
Peterborough
PE2 9BF
Telephone: 01733 890066
Website: www.youngwriters.co.uk

FOREWORD

Survival Log: Day 52

We had almost lost hope. Disasters befell the earth and chaos reigned; we didn't think there were many survivors, if any. Here at Young Writers we sent out a call, a signal to anyone out there to communicate and let us know that we weren't alone. It seemed like a lost cause.

But then something miraculous happened.

We received thousands of messages – tales of destruction and danger, stories of survival against the odds, and devastating accounts of disasters both natural and man-made wreaking havoc upon the land. Not all of them have a happy ending, but all of them offer a blazing beacon of hope that secondary school pupils across the land are keeping their creativity alive.

Communications had to be kept to 100 words, but even with this restraint they've created vivid descriptions, powerful imagery and epic tales of the fight for survival; the fight for humanity. These stories have been collected in this anthology to serve as a lasting record of the chaos that raged across the globe, and how we fought back.

Every author featured should be proud in the vital part they've played in creating these Survival Sagas. I declare Mission Chaos a success.

Signing off,

Catherine

CONTENTS

Harry Clist (12) 60
Mason Devlin (11) 61
Emily Checkley (12) 62
Jemima Dewey (12) 63

Marden High School, North Shields

Sophie Mia Harman (11) 64
Taylor Alexandra Leadbitter (11) 65
Matthew Maley (11) 66
Charlotte Ainscow (11) 67
Jonathan Maley (11) 68
Haydon Piercy (11) 69
Rory Pattinson (11) 70
Cerys Carle (12) 71
Heather Marchbank (11) 72
Dillon Stephen Burgess (11) 73
Jessica Hoolison (11) 74
Jonny Rushent (11) 75
Elizabeth Shannon (12) 76
Rowan Bennett (11) 77
Harley Jay Leslie (11) 78
Jack Shorting (11) 79
Lewis Burton (11) 80
Alesha Assam (11) 81
Amara Jessica Rawlings (11) 82
Libby Alice Shaw (11) 83
Eisha Sikka (11) 84
Gabriel Knox (12) 85
Ruben Parnell (11) 86
Josie Elizabeth Bowmaker (11) 87
Hollie Lawson Mills (11) 88
Jennifer Stutt 89
Molly Ballard (11) 90
Rory O'Neill (12) 91
Luke Brown (11) 92
Harry James Wallace (12) 93
Samuel Rushent (11) 94
Jayda Kershaw (11) 95
Taylor Walker (11) 96
Tom George Warne (11) 97
Malachi Taylor (11) 98
Macey McKean (11) 99

Philippa Springle (11) 100
Thomas Armstrong (11) 101
Francesca Herzberg (11) 102
Andrew Joseph Scott (11) 103
Alexis Jane Elliott (11) 104
Lily Rose Hobkirk (11) 105
Charlie David Gilchrist (11) 106
Chloe Hadland (10) 107
Jake Waddell (11) 108
Olivia Taylor Appleby (11) 109
Freya Elizabeth Yare (11) 110
Isla Hodgson (11) 111
Emmeline Law (11) 112
Thomas Dennis Russell (11) 113
Lucas Bell (11) 114
Joseph McAvelia (11) 115
Erin Leanne Goicoechea (11) 116
Connie Yeomans (11) 117
Lilly Hunter (11) 118
William Ridsdale (11) 119
Ryan Nolan (11) 120
Finley Taylor (11) 121
Daniel Robert Grieveson (11) 122
Adyan Ahmed (11) 123
Joseph Gilmour (11) 124
Eve Thomas (11) 125
Isabelle Hannant (11) 126
Matthew Aust (11) 127
Alexander Slaven (11) 128
Jack Wardlaw (11) 129
Aaron Karaboga (11) 130
Jack 131
Jack Sutherland (11) 132
Malaika Souza (11) 133
Holly Howells (11) 134
Molly Dowse (11) 135
Emma Melvin (11) 136
Olivia May Chaplow (11) 137
Sandy Bainton (11) 138
Preben Koldal (11) 139
Ankitha Ramesh (11) 140
Emma Jammeh (11) 141
Nathan Potts (11) 142

Zachary Cook (10)	143	Paige McMichael (12)	183
Chloe Shanks (11)	144	Aimee Eloise Bruce (13)	184
Thomas Ratcliffe (11)	145	Jorge Martin (14)	185
Esme Robb (11)	146	Courtney Spencer (13)	186
Oscar George Richardson (11)	147	Holly Bainbridge (12)	187
Gracie Pears (11)	148	Katie Elizabeth Daniels (12)	188
Erin McEntee (11)	149	Daniel Dent (13)	189
Will Jones (11)	150	Kallumn Cooley (12)	190
Jasmine Lily Lee (11)	151	Ahmed Raheem Ali (13)	191
Hajar Al-Sabbahy (11)	152	Jessica Sawyer (11)	192
Libby Bilcliffe (11)	153	Thomas Reese (13)	193
Olivia Watson (11)	154	Ellie-May Riley Caygill (12)	194
Liam Skipsey (11)	155	Hollie Wright (13)	195
Jonathan Lawson Mills (11)	156	Ryan Walton (14)	196
William Clarkson (11)	157	Toni Leigh Palmer (13)	197
Tilly Smith (11)	158	Jamie Day (12)	198
Harry Jacob Short (11)	159	Matthew Dunn (12)	199
Hayden Dunning (11)	160	Jacob Stanford (12)	200
Ava Lauren Taylor (11)	161	Katie Louise Dixon (13)	201
Isla Russell (11)	162	Krish Kumar (13)	202
Ella McKean (11)	163		
Luke Robert Potts (11)	164		
Jamie Dunn (12)	165		
Charlie Chambers (11)	166		
Jack Harker (11)	167		
Cameron Alexander Ross (11)	168		

Wyvern Academy, Eggleston View

Mae Withrow (12)	169
Faith Parry (12)	170
Isaac Matthew Marlow (12)	171
Connie Ward (14)	172
Libby Graham (12)	173
Joshua Baker (13)	174
Amber Grace Matthews (13)	175
Louis Lee Jenkinson (12)	176
Caitlan Morrison (11)	177
Thomas Klein (12)	178
Brandon Nicholson (11)	179
Daniel Metcalfe (13)	180
Jack Gibson (13)	181
Arman Ahmed (13)	182

THE
MINI SAGAS

Why?

It was daunting. My hands were clenched together and my knees were stuck on the ground, requesting help. No matter how hard I tried, I had no stamina whatsoever to do anything about it.
Bang!
"Oww!"
Bang!
"Oww!"
My feelings twisted around each other and formed confusion and hatred. Why me? Why us? My heart broke into a million pieces while I realised not only would we die, so would the babies. The poor innocent babies. What did they do to deserve this? We reached a camp which read: 'Concentration camp, where you will meet your friend, Death...'

Hibah Ahmed (12)
Brampton Manor Academy, East Ham

A Visit From Death

The machines march; the war has begun... A massacre awaits the citizens. Floods of bullets erupt from the guns with velocity. The victims feel steel slice past their skin, its cold, rigid texture aggravates their trepidation. Blood flings itself into the air, pervading it with a pungent stench of debris. The Grim Reaper has arrived. The men, women and children of this world slowly feel agony clench them. Their lungs sting as their hunger for oxygen escalates. Their ears are no longer able to detect decibels, just a long, screeching silence until death steals what's his from their chest.

Adeniel David (12)
Brampton Manor Academy, East Ham

Silence

The screams outside fall silent... we're all huddled in the bunker together. It's really dirty and damp as it is underground. Me, my sister and my parents are patiently waiting for it all to just end. But the thing is, we don't know that this war won't end anytime soon. The screams are muffled by the ground above us, so are the explosions. There's seldom space for us and we can barely even breathe, it's very hard to. We're all sweating bullets, from both fear and warmth. We don't even know what's even happening out there. We can only imagine.

Snehita Gupta (11)

Brampton Manor Academy, East Ham

Silence

We couldn't make a sound. They were all around us. The green saliva was on the walls, dripping casually on the floor. Then it happened. There were fast-paced footsteps all around us. I couldn't see a thing. The shadows felt like they were creeping up on us. My head darted around the room when... I could see it. I signalled to my terrified friends.
"Go!" I screamed as loud as I could.
Thousands of eyes widened and the room filled up with screams. I opened the door. It almost ripped off the wall.
"I made it!"
I was alone.

Archie Mowles (12)
Brampton Manor Academy, East Ham

My Young Adolescence...

Beep! Beep! "Check his heart rate, check his pulse."
My parents all tearful, were not allowed behind the
curtains. I was put asleep, not knowing what was
happening in the real world. My head was in the
clouds, soaring endlessly away from my real life.
Today, I was being fitted for the 'new way of life'...
Marmalization. All my life, nothing had pleased me.
Being and becoming a young adolescent was a
struggle, all was a struggle. This was a way to fix
me a permanent smile.
"David Finch, follow me to this room..."

Louie Pilbrow (11)
Brampton Manor Academy, East Ham

Wi-Fi Crisis

The silence outside fell to screams. How could such a wonderful and peaceful household of happiness turn into such a disaster? A black screen would appear, ticking and ticking like a Wi-Fi bomb about to explode in people's houses. Suddenly, an expected scream appeared.

"Oh dear lord, how could you do this to me? The foul practice has turned itself upon me, like a cruel flash of hell!

Now here I lie, never to rise again. My rubbish network is to blame for such sadness upon my life."

Who knew that Wi-Fi could be such a sad priority?

Charlee Fisher (11)
Brampton Manor Academy, East Ham

Tap, Tap Under The Bed

Tap! Tap! I heard. I rolled my eyes around the room, looking for the suspicious sound. Nothing. I went back to my YouTube video which I was more keen on. The lights began to flicker until darkness shrouded the room. The intimidating howls of the wind outside made the tapping faster, as I held onto my blanket tightly. Slowly, I started to realise the tapping came from under the bed! The temptation of looking under my bed made my body shudder. I looked under my bed and saw a black, deep hole.
Tap! Tap! and it was all sinister, dark.

Harshita Somra (11)
Brampton Manor Academy, East Ham

Day Of The Dark

I sprinted swiftly, taking rapid glimpses behind me. All I saw was the islands gradually parting from each other whilst the thunder shook the ground as if Zeus had jumped down from Olympus. The ground I was running on started to rise. I gripped my hands and sprinted as fast as my legs could go until... I heard a voice whisper, "It's alright, just let go with the calming breeze!"

My head started racing as if my blood vessels were fighting an unordinary disease. Automatically, I... I just let go. I just plunged into complete, utter darkness.

Mohammed Yaseen Saif Miah (12)
Brampton Manor Academy, East Ham

Gunshot

There I was, running. Running to a place I didn't know. Screams flooded my ears. I felt like I was the ground that was getting trampled over. A huge group of us turned to a corner where there was a dead end.

"Hush!" a man whispered.

A feeling of relief washed through me and then the baby started crying. Oh, the baby started crying. In seconds, there were a series of gunshots in the distance. Then a sharp, short, deafening scream. I turned my head around, when a small yet brutal force jerked my head back. Then everything went black...

Sarah Rudaina (11)

Brampton Manor Academy, East Ham

Time Is Running Out

After the smoke cleared, I heard me crying, shouting and screaming. Everyone was running and panicking. I was looking, looking for my family and friends but all I found was a man. He told me to run away from this place before 'they' get me. I tried to ask him why but he kept shouting to run! I started running and he kept shouting to run.
"Run faster! They're looking for you!"
I started crying after running for about ten minutes. I couldn't find my family and I didn't know where I was.

Arora Rowja (12)
Brampton Manor Academy, East Ham

Looped

Listen to me, I don't have much time to explain but please, just hear me out. There is this guy who chases me down and murders me. Over and over again. I don't know anything about this guy at all but when he kills me, my day restarts and the only way I can end my suffering is if I find his identity and kill him.

Damn! I can hear him coming. Sorry, I've got to go or else I'm going to, you know... die! I'll explain if we meet again, okay? You can count on it, just trust me!

Zaid Nawsath (12)
Brampton Manor Academy, East Ham

The Eruption

The volcano spat and shot out molten meteors, while my friend and I had seen a bunker. My friend had suggested to run there but it would be a risky move. We saw that the eruption had paused. We made a run for it, sprinting rapidly. As soon as the bunker had closed, a meteor shot the wall but we'd dodged it. We had seen an electro bunker, all futuristic, and we played video games and had fun. We both started to get hungry. We looked at the fridge and it was empty. We began to look at each other...

Niamul Islam (11)

Brampton Manor Academy, East Ham

Danger Zone

The apocalypse was roaring in rage, we started to run. As we stopped to rest, a piece of metal flew across and hit my brother. For a moment, I froze still. I was shaking and I broke down into tears as he was my last family member living. He was leaning against a tree, trying to support his own body weight. His gasps of pain were like knives stabbing me. This was the danger zone, not the safe zone. In the end, the world did not end in one bang or a whisper, but rather one scream at a time.

Alexandrina Macovei (12)

Brampton Manor Academy, East Ham

It's Time

The machines marched; the war had begun... It was a crazy, no one dared to help but would dare to kill. The whole land was full of blood. Nobody was able to live for too long. It was horrible. I was left alone, my father and mother were killed. My brother and I were spared but when I turned, I was to get killed but then he took the risk and left me. I hoped that I could've been there for him like he was for me but I was happy because I was finally seeing him. Goodbye, my friend...

Nasma Farjana Hossain (12)
Brampton Manor Academy, East Ham

Destroyed

The smoke clears! We aren't prepared. The noise of the bomb is still ringing in my ears. What can I do? I look at the rest, eyes shut and goosebumps wrinkling their skin. I pluck up the courage and look at what used to be my home. I can't bear the pain so I shut my eyes again. The rest open their eyes, to find the horror of what used to be my home, our home. I close my eyes so as not to bear the pain anymore. Then the noise of another bomb floods into my ears again. Why?

Lila Bartholomew (12)
Brampton Manor Academy, East Ham

Alone

I was the only one left. I had ten tins of beans. The floor was flooded. I felt the water flood in my shoe. There was no one to talk to, no one to help. I fell asleep.

When I woke up, I felt mindless but then it flooded back to me. I was alone. The food was about to finish. I was going to restrict myself to one tin a day so it would last longer but when I went to get my daily tin, the wave came in again. It demolished my bunk and I had nothing...

Oladimeji Ayomide Amusan (11)
Brampton Manor Academy, East Ham

From Dust

The world burned. After the disaster and disease that humanity had survived through, chaos reigned! Raiders scoured the globe, searching for anything they could use, any settlements to ruin. Humanity was fighting for its survival, but its main enemy was itself! The future seemed bleak. But, in humanity's darkest hour, the Union emerged from the shadows. After building up its strength for years, we were finally ready to launch our assault! We brought salvation to those without hope and brought technology and sophistication from before the current time of strife. The Union would take back our world, no matter what...

Robert Hayles (13)

Christ The King College, Carisbrooke

Insane Silence

Silence. Could you put a sound to silence? Writing this, I could've heard the screams from the tower, that dreaded place where they were all taken. I could've heard the minutely quiet echoes of the guns fired during the nine minutes. I shudder if I remember it. I could've heard the footsteps echoing from the tunnels below, where they tried to hide. I could've heard the water dripping down endlessly from the dank, mossy walls. I could've heard her screams when it- I'll gloss over that. It was all so loud, so corrupting, yet quiet! So painfully quiet.

Peter Andrew Abbott (13)

Christ The King College, Carisbrooke

Follow The Leader

"Follow me," it whispered. "Follow me."
I felt like I was underground in a coffin. The voice was deep, croaky, like an old man. My heart skipped a beat. My spine tingled! Where was I? Was I buried alive? I was in a coffin! Repeatedly, I knocked on the box, eager to come out. Finally, someone's footsteps became louder and louder, until I heard someone unlocking a chain! Had I been kidnapped? Some mysterious figure opened the lid of the box. All I could see were wide grins, glowing red eyes and matted black hair! *I'm going to die...*

Lexie Harverson (12)
Christ The King College, Carisbrooke

Last Nights

It has been nine years since the outbreak started. Things haven't got better. Each month goes by and we notice that the infected are hunting instead of wandering. They even attack each other! We've noticed that they can climb without a scratch. Some have got larger. We get more scared as each day goes by! I even saw one throw a car at another! Unfortunately, the same fate met one of our scavengers. We were caught off guard. He couldn't defend himself! Same as usual, if anyone finds this, I'm probably dead.
Signed, Captain Fox.

Tyron Fox (12)
Christ The King College, Carisbrooke

The Unusual Silence

The screams outside fell silent. I was the only person left! Something rang repeatedly. What was it? Where was it coming from? I ran to the bunker. The light disappeared with every step I took. I didn't take a step back. My heart pounded. My breathing was getting faster and faster every second. I waited. The silence was unusual. It was usually shrieks from every direction possible! I closed my eyes for a second or two. As I opened them, a light shone at my eyes! It illuminated hundreds of figures stood right before me. This is how I died...

Jasmine Witton (12)
Christ The King College, Carisbrooke

The Black Cloud Of People

It never stops! I'm the only one left. The black cloud gets everyone, including my family! An echoing alarm rings through the city and shatters the glass. It smashes as all the possessed people roam around the city's parking lots, shops and houses! My hearing is always on alert and my eyes widen in fear. My heart beats fast. No one knows how the black cloud got out and I definitely don't want to find out! The black cloud runs around biting people, then they turn in less than ten minutes! It is now my mission to stay alive...

Karmen Hirst (12)

Christ The King College, Carisbrooke

Blood, Sweat And Tears

Velvet fluid runs down my sliced forehead and it drips like a tap down my blistered nose. Popped blisters soak in sweat like a parched sponge. I feel my eyes flutter but I force myself to keep them open as salty drops roll down my non-existent cheeks! A gust of arid breeze stalks in-between my ragged clothes that lie on my lifeless body. I feel my heartbeat slow down and my pulse slowly becomes an echo as my skin represents stagnant snow. I glance up one last time as I slowly lose consciousness; I know they'll find a cure...

Guillianne Ponferrada (12)

Christ The King College, Carisbrooke

Dead Or Alive?

Darkness smothered me until I lost all consciousness. I was unable to picture anything in my mind. Suddenly, I was back in the war zone except... I was alone. Regaining balance, I stood up and listened for any sign of life. Nothing. No missiles, no bombs, no gut-wrenching screams of terror! It was like the whole human race had vanished, leaving me behind. My mind was racing and I was slowly losing sense of my surroundings. As I attempted to work out this horrific puzzle, it finally hit me. *I might not even be alive...*

Ellie-May Rose Hopkins (14)
Christ The King College, Carisbrooke

Eruption

All I remember is crawling under my bed as the molten lava dripped around me. I heard my mother's screams but my body was fixed in position. I looked on in horror as my sister's lifeless body fell down next to my door! My dad pushed under the burning timber of wood into my room. He grabbed hold of my wrists and we waddled over to the window! We heard muffled screams and as Dad opened it, we hopped out! I couldn't believe the sight of the street as Mrs Herrimoore grabbed her cat and shuffled to the fire engine...

Jacob Sprooles (14)

Christ The King College, Carisbrooke

The End

The town is empty and abandoned. No one would believe that the streets were once filled with people. I am one of the few who survived the virus, but I can't celebrate yet. There are still zombies out there! It is 2030 and I have found a camp! They are helping me get resources and fight off the zombies. We can't hold them off much longer. They're getting in through the walls. They have already killed five out of the seven of us! We are all going to turn in the end. There's no point in fighting them off...

Oliver Harrison (13)
Christ The King College, Carisbrooke

Help Me

Where? Where do I go? Where do I hide? I'm scared, I just want this to end. Everywhere I look, the sky and Earth are just... exploding. It's like I'm stuck in a never-ending nightmare. Run! I should run, as far and as fast as my legs will carry me. I am ready to bolt through the front door but my legs won't stop trembling! My throat is closing up and my salty tears are blinding me. I search deep down and find enough courage to stand outside. The sky is falling! The world is ending. Please, help me...

Daisy Philpott (12)
Christ The King College, Carisbrooke

It Is Time To Give Up

It's been over a year. The storm rushing towards us. Black figures in thick smoke, screaming and running through obstacles trying to have a taste of our fresh flesh! It was unspeakable to say how many of these mutants were cruising through the city. These mutants have intelligence, they use each other to climb walls, building nearly everything! This all wouldn't have happened if Doctor S Harrison didn't try to test cures on prisoners! The world has changed and it's now turned into big chaos...

Curtis Allen (13)
Christ The King College, Carisbrooke

Death Row

Arm cut off, the pain was unbearable. There were too many! I tried as hard as I could but it was too late. He was transformed into a butcher, a mangled monster so big he could eat a three-storey house! There were only three minutes until we were going to be attacked by the horde. We had no chance unless we killed the leader. The thing making this happen. We headed towards its cave but they launched their attack! I watched my friend be cut in half and eaten! The last thing I saw... "Arghhh!"

Keaton Magee (13)

Christ The King College, Carisbrooke

The End Is Coming

The machines marched; the war had begun! I knew there was no turning back. I couldn't destroy them by myself so I had to ask my friend Murlin. This man knew so many things about war, he even knew some of the strategies from World War Two! So me and him were going to be the bravest people ever. We took them on one by one, watching their heads roll onto the floor! They were then all dead except one, the mega one. Its name was The Machine King. As I stormed forwards towards it, I tripped...

William Lakin (13)
Christ The King College, Carisbrooke

The Last Survival

We were on our last legs, barely holding on for our lives. For once, we all thought it was the end! My legs were shaking, they felt like jelly. We were all on our last rations! We could all hear the torturing noises coming from outside. I didn't believe I could do this. Every word I said, I stuttered with pure fear. The ominous clouds looked down at me as I shouted, "God, please help me!"

All of a sudden, we heard a loud bang and we were all so terrified for our lives...

Brooke Faith Moss-Simmonds (12)

Christ The King College, Carisbrooke

Eyes

All was silent. A blazing sun broke the darkness. The war had ended. Silence engulfed me and my thoughts. A cold substance oozed slowly across my battered face. A scream awoke me from my deep slumber! I slowly stood up, edging my way to the opening of my patchwork tent. Before me, I saw a land of fright and terror, a story of tragedy echoed around the scene. I saw Charlotte lying spread-eagled on the ground, the last look of terror still etched upon her face! Her empty eyes still haunt me.

Mabel Hayward (13)
Christ The King College, Carisbrooke

Will I Survive?

Everyone has gone. That's all I know. Well... I know how it started. I was stuck in a dark room with no doors or windows and all I could hear was the sound of strong winds bringing a storm. Everyone had left by this point, but I didn't listen and now I wish that I had. I was stuck in the room for what seemed like weeks and when all my worry bottled up inside of me. I knew I had to find a way out. This is where it's left me - fighting for my life. Will I survive?

Grace Flynn (13)
Christ The King College, Carisbrooke

Man-Eating Zombies

I wake up to more open sores eating away at my skin! The world is coming to an end. There are only a few survivors with no water, no food and no supplies to survive. There are only zombies looking for open wounds and flesh to feast on! There are millions of man-eating zombies and only a few lonely survivors scattered across what was once our world but is now a lava-filled hell hole filled with misery! The world has turned into chaos... *How will I survive this?*

Eloise Wall (14)
Christ The King College, Carisbrooke

Prophecy

I felt my heart skip a beat. I always knew I was different, but I never thought I was *that* different.
"Years ago, I was told of a prophecy," the old woman rasped. "Of a half-blooded child- "
"Half-blooded? What do you mean half-blooded?" I whispered, my eyes clouded with confusion.
"Half-human, half-spirit."
"But that's impossible!"
"Hush!" she paused before continuing. "She was destined to destroy the human race. She was thrown from a waterfall. They tried to kill her first - however, it seems you couldn't be killed that easily..."
She reached to her pocket...

Darcie Windsor (12)

Felpham Community College, Felpham

Mission Chaos

I ran.

They ran.

I turned.

They turned.

Buzzz! The counter clicked over. Another had gone. Fifteen left.

Chaos was an understatement. Everything around me was gradually burning to black smithereens. This ash city was once New York.

No humans for miles, just robots, the ones hunting us down, the fifteen survivors. Now, I was sprawled across the evilly cold floor of an underground bunker, breathing scarily heavily. Me and everyone else's future depended on my next actions. I couldn't run forever. They were faster; I would die. I was already going that way.

What was I supposed to do...?

Josie Kelly (12)
Felpham Community College, Felpham

Edge Of The World

Ella was on the edge of the world. People were falling into the chasm. She couldn't save them. She was helpless.

"Demigod!" roared the Titan.

Ella knew she couldn't defeat him. She swung herself up, glaring at the Titan.

"You should kill me," she said.

He looked confused. "I don't take orders from demigods!"

He charged and she jumped out of the way - but not quick enough. He grabbed her. Everyone was dead. The world was chaos! He squeezed her. She screamed...!

She woke up, realising it wasn't a dream - it was a memory of her past...

Summer Polman (12)

Felpham Community College, Felpham

Mission Chaos

"How can I stop this chaos from spreading? I need to find a way..."

The year's 2054. Chaos has taken over the world. Joe Zussman decided to go search for survivors. Joe found an old house which looked abandoned, but he heard noise coming from it.

"Hello? Is anyone here? This place gives me the creeps..."

Suddenly, Joe saw a strange figure under the stairs. The person he saw was just a child.

"Who are you?" said the child.

"I'm Joe. I'm here to stop the chaos."

Then Joe got to the core, destroyed it and saved the new world.

Alexander Marshall (12)

Felpham Community College, Felpham

The Beginning Of The End!

Crash! Bang! It's all you can hear at the moment. Nothing will be the same again but that doesn't mean nothing will change. Darkness engulfs us as the days go on. Everything has ended, everything has gone. What's happening here is the unthinkable, the world has gone up in flames. No one can survive. No one wants to. Everything here is death and death takes everything in its way without hesitation. Abandoned, forgotten, isolated. That's everyone here and that's how it will end unless the light can keep shining, unless people can keep fighting, unless change happens soon...

Sally Atkins (13)

Felpham Community College, Felpham

The Destruction Of Humanity

"So, some guy hates humans and destroyed humanity. So, everything was normal and then there was an explosion. *Boom!* I looked in the other direction. *Pow!* The guy stored bombs in everyday items all over the world. I know you're wondering what I did. I ran and then something must've hit me on the head because I fell unconscious for a while.

I woke up and I was looking at the rubble. No Burger King, no street, no perfect Italian cuisine. Now I'm just chilling in some arcade. I feel like I shouldn't be talking to a vending machine..."

Luke George Hobbs (13)
Felpham Community College, Felpham

Plant Attack

Twenty years ago, I was procrastinating about my art homework by watching TV. I started to hear noises and I looked out of my window to see a bunch of walking plants slaughtering innocent people. The roads were full of blood and guts. Suddenly, a plant looked and made a high-pitched screech and I saw at least fifty plants circling my house and charging at it. Then nothing happened because they were plants. They started taking down the door. The barged in and started smashing everything downstairs until they barged upstairs, looking for me. Then they barged into my room...

Alexander Decarteret (13)

Felpham Community College, Felpham

The Shockwave

The flash blinded the weak-eyed. The sound deafened the elderly. Mushroom-like clouds surrounded everything in my sight. The ground shook. I ran inside and checked the radio. All I could hear was something about ex-Cold War bombs detonating. Sirens echoed around the whole area, loud screams shattered the windows throughout the village. I stayed inside, putting my fingers in my ears to block out the horrible bangs that were going on across the world, not just my local area. The shockwave came towards my house. I knew my time was up. I shut my eyes and prayed I wouldn't die.

Olly Hobbs (13)
Felpham Community College, Felpham

Run

The world has come to an end. We walk along beside one another. We observe the obstacles around us, everything destroyed: homes, shopping, anything you can think of is gone.

As we walk past the ruins of buildings, we visualise what it was like before it started, before family died in front of us; staying dead for minutes, then coming back as a new person, forgetting every memory created, bloodthirsty for anything in sight; having to run for our lives, feeling the most scared we'd ever been, but then feeling guilty and ill from running away from family...

Helena Wilson (12)
Felpham Community College, Felpham

The End Of All Things

It all happened so quickly. One minute we were having a lovely family dinner and, the next, *boom!* It was the end of the world as we knew it. They crawled out of the broken ground with no intentions except to kill and eat.

We're the only people left, twelve of us. We're doomed. We're going to die! The bloodcurdling screams of all my friends being brutally slaughtered sends shivers down my spine. That's it, it's my turn. The monster grabs me but, suddenly, drops me and tumbles to the ground. *Bang!* He was shot, but by who?

Ruby Donohue (13)
Felpham Community College, Felpham

Rebecca's Diary

I can't believe how an invention that we humans had discovered could stab us in the back. We spent years creating a new phenomenon, robots. After achieving that, we wanted to improve it. Now, here we are; some dead, some barely alive, trying to hide from the robots that are aiming to destroy all humanity and take over the world. There are only several thousand humans breathing and I'm one of them. I'm keeping out of sight in an abandoned school with my friends. Our resources are low, food, water, a few weapons. Wait, I have to go... It's them!

Raghavi Pakirathan-Kandasamy

Felpham Community College, Felpham

The Terror That Awaits

For six months straight, I didn't leave my home. I was too petrified to finally face the havoc that the lethal virus had caused to humanity and the town I adored. But, now, finally, I was out. Terror seeped through me. The corpses of people I'd known all my life laid scattered on the mountains of rubble like pieces of Lego. They all had grey, patchy skin and sunken, dead eyes. It sent a shiver down my spine. What had caused this terrible tragedy? I became observant. Then I noticed it. Empty chocolate wrappers littered the place I'd called home.

Ruby Hobbs (13)
Felpham Community College, Felpham

Mission Chaos

My heart was beating so fast. I was shaking a lot. Lasers sizzled through people as they ran for their lives! More and more shot out of the enemy's gun, blocking doors and windows, trapping people. There was the piercing sound of screaming...

All of a sudden, smoke started to appear out of every crevice in the walls, floor and ceiling. People began falling to their deaths. You could hardly see a thing!

That was the moment when I realised I was the only one left. The screams fell silent outside. The silence was painful. It was just me now...

Gracie-Mae Cox

Felpham Community College, Felpham

Hacked

I sat there, staring out into the unforgiving wasteland that was New York. Leaking from every wall, speaker and phone, the ringing noise that was the hypnosis felt like a constant buzz of an insect in my ear.

Bang! For a split second, the ringing stopped. I froze in fear, thinking of what just happened. Had they got bombs? What could've made such a loud noise?

Rushing to the window, I shut my curtains and got a glimpse of the chaos that was happening! I didn't know what was happening - all I knew was that I might not survive...

Gracie Scopes (14)

Felpham Community College, Felpham

Darkness Fell

Bang! Darkness fell. It became extremely cold. The wind whipped past my face and made my eyes water uncontrollably. What happened? Why was it night? I didn't have answers. I had to find out what happened to the sun. Now!

As I headed back home, I thought to myself, *my book!* It turned night to day but I lost it before the end. I needed to know what happened. I couldn't... I didn't want to believe this. The moon shone brightly on something glistening. Should I go and see if it was to do with the disappearance of the sun...

Erin Eddey (13)
Felpham Community College, Felpham

Horizon

Traumatising memories flood through my head;
the damage the destruction, the chaos...
I walked down to the beach, probably for the last
time in my life, and stared at the ocean, the ocean
that destroyed the human race. I looked out the
corner of my eye. A lifeless body lay frozen on the
ground. I felt like a planet lost in its own universe. I
remember gazing at the horizon - that's when I
saw it. The wave came closer. The wind began
howling like a wolf...
A tsunami, the monster everyone had dreaded.
Was this what they called the end...?

Annelise Mai Mezzone (12)
Felpham Community College, Felpham

Questions

My heart was racing. I didn't dare breath. The lights were flashing now, leaving me in the darkness. Spiders were eating me alive, my neck aching from being stuffed in an old, musky cupboard.

Suddenly, it happened so fast, the door flung open. Two men grabbed me, one with a cigarette in his mouth, the other with missing teeth and a knife in his hand! It was covered with dripping fresh blood. I was thrown onto a chair and tied so tight it cut into my wrists and ankles, making them turn purple. They screamed at me, "Where is he?"

Katie Harris (12)
Felpham Community College, Felpham

It's Over

Solar flares had wreaked havoc on the Earth only a few days ago. I haven't found any survivors, just me and my dog. Buildings have collapsed and fire has spread, as did the panicked screams the night it happened. It's burned in my mind. Every single second. The screams, the tears, the screeches as buildings collapsed.

Now, it's eerily quiet. The crackling flames and my own footsteps make me uneasy. There is no one here. It's just us, all on our own, possibly forever. It's all over. Nothing will ever be the same again...

Jennifer Hackett (12)
Felpham Community College, Felpham

Mission Chaos

Alex listened to the waves crashing against the shoreline while seagulls flew above, searching for food. The sun beamed on his face and he wished he had worn a hat. He walked the beach, the hot sand stinging his toes. Boats sailed in the distance and he wondered what it would feel like to be free of land - but that thought dissipated. His mind shifted to when he almost drowned in the ocean. Suddenly, a flaming meteor came out of the sky; this was no ordinary meteor, it made the ground shake like an earthquake. The city sirens went on...

Yevgeniy Kagarov (12)
Felpham Community College, Felpham

Mission Chaos

Death, destruction... I'm on the brink of death; the infection has finally got to me. The poison runs through me like acid, but I'm on the brink of success. It's been fifty-four days finding my way through the labyrinth of time. I'm going back in time to stop it from happening, this timeline. Victory shines upon me, but then my skin starts to melt like ice on a hot day. I have one minute to live! I dash for the machine and, with my last breath, activate the machine, saving this sad, doomed timeline. I die victorious...

Dylan Channell
Felpham Community College, Felpham

The War

Guns blew and I was scared to death. My heart kept on one speed and that was a million miles per hour! My best friend stood at my side as we fought the mad war that had struck near the end of the world disaster.

"We're going to be safe as long as we just keep our post."

I twirled the necklace that Mum had given me when she died. It was a good luck charm.

"For Earth!" shouted my best friend as she ran out. After hours of fighting, we won and the human race rebuilt their civilisation...

Bethany Anne Mary Bolton (12)

Felpham Community College, Felpham

Taken Over

Now we are at the end, the human race has faced terrible trials and tribulations to reach Mission Chaos. The few that are left now fight for survival, resources and land. Our world has been taken over by the Autriax, a refugee from the planet Foutra, who came here to enslave us and find the Skaurus Shell, the most powerful substance in the universe. It is said to be able to make the one who has it immortal and unstoppable. Although, if the wielder is not worthy, they shall be destroyed and the shell will go back into hiding.

Charlie-George Shadbolt (12)
Felpham Community College, Felpham

Mission Chaos

Bang! Everything suddenly fell silent. The war had begun. There were two groups fighting for land, Team A and Team B. I was part of Team A, fighting for this land. At this point, things started to get out of hand. All my mates were dropping dead here and there. Before I knew it, I was the last man standing for my team.

We were the only ones left. It all came down to this. I was about to shoot my gun when a bright light burst from the horizon.

Boom!

Me and my enemy were shot stone dead...

Ruby-May Rainey (12)
Felpham Community College, Felpham

Mission Chaos

My heart raced in my chest as I felt her hand slip out of mine. She was gone. A tear rushed down my face, stinging as the salty water touched my burnt cheek. I pulled myself off the ground, afraid to look into the gaping hole in front of me. *One wrong move*, I thought. I watched as he pushed past the terrified women and children. When I looked closer, I saw something: his leg bone was completely exposed. With that, I collapsed...

When I awoke, I saw that I was in a cramped safety bunker. I would survive...

Lucy Lennox (11)
Felpham Community College, Felpham

Safe Zone

Hi, my name's Gary. I don't have much time so I'm gonna keep this quick. Three days ago, continents all over the world started disappearing, flooding the rest of the world. I live in Manchester and have a little appliance ship here. I was gathering supplies from the fridge in the break room when I got signal on my phone. I was told I only had twenty-four hours to get to Antartica, the only safe zone, because they had put barricades up before it flooded. Now all that I have to do is... Wait. What's that?

Connor Simmonds (13)

Felpham Community College, Felpham

What Will Happen Next?

They were a week into the war and so far, neither team was winning. There had been acid splashed, guns shot, and that was all Bob the cook heard 24/7. He cooked the food for the soldiers and it was a very dangerous job. He could get anything thrown at him, but there was still a worse job. Jeff the soldier was on the front line. He had everything thrown at him.

Tuesday, most of the soldiers were tired - but then a pipe full of acid exploded and everyone was dying and burning! The land was melting away slowly...

Harry Clist (12)
Felpham Community College, Felpham

Mission Chaos

I woke as if it was an emergency, like sleeping was dangerous. Trees torn down, houses burnt... this was all my fault. I started sobbing, my tears dropping into the void. I tried to imagine being back in California, the sun beaming, the delicious ice cream - but there was no time to sit back and think. I had to find a way to get back to Earth. I was on the planet Protocol23YX, which was known for its terrible air quality. I needed a way home, fast. But at that same moment, it dawned on me. I was stranded. Forever.

Mason Devlin (11)

Felpham Community College, Felpham

The Lost Plane

The very last survivors look for help, searching everywhere. There's nothing to be seen for miles, just open fields going on forever. All you can hear are the horrifying sounds of people screaming and shouting, desperate to find a single piece of life. Now we are settled here with less and less people each day. Each one goes to try and find something out there, but no one ever comes back. Everyone in our community is happy where we are now and no one has any record of the outside world and never will...

Emily Checkley (12)
Felpham Community College, Felpham

Mission Chaos

There were flames bursting out of the ground! It was almost like I was at the core of the Earth! I was the last one left. I had lost everything. Agonising screams passed through my mind. I was in such pain. This had to end now. I eased myself up. It was like my whole body was throbbing, but I had to regain all the strength I had.

As I stood there, sweating and panting, I saw the outline of a dark figure. They got closer. I realised it was him all along. He had crimson stains all over him...

Jemima Dewey (12)
Felpham Community College, Felpham

Heavens Against The Underworld

"Hades, give up now, our alliance has beaten most of your undead army," boomed Zeus.

"No brother, we shall see who wins at the end of an elemental battle, fire versus lightning. That's my offer," claimed Hades.

"Deal, brother," Zeus said.

They were on Earth, a human planet. They were surrounded by destroyed buildings, screaming people and the sky was cloudy above them. The brothers battled with the elements of fire and lightning.

"Give up now!" said Hades.

"Never!" shouted Zeus.

They ran, using their extremely dangerous powers. They collided and the world went dark. A huge, loud explosion occurred...

Sophie Mia Harman (11)
Marden High School, North Shields

Death

"It's coming closer," I whispered. A black, mysterious cloud, that's what it was. A liquid cloud struck death to anyone blocking its path.

"I think we should run," whispered Wilbur, dropping down his gun and turn to face me.

"What?" I screamed, not realising how loud I was.

"Well, we tried and tried. I think we can't defeat this awful creature," he explained.

I felt angry and upset, a tear rolled down my face, "B-b-but how could you?" I shouted. A few more tears ran down. Then I burst into tears and ran off screaming of death. *Bang!*

Taylor Alexandra Leadbitter (11)

Marden High School, North Shields

Is It The End?

Only four people were left on Planet Earth. Mark and his three friends only had apples because everything had been infected by the mysterious aliens...

Four days had passed and unfortunately, Philip died. They were running out of places to live that hadn't been infected, even places that weren't infected were haunted by the dead. Luckily, there was a bunker hidden in the leaves.

"Safe at last," yelled Mark.

Day after day, Simon and Finley started getting weaker. After two dreadful weeks, both friends hadn't risen from their sleep. Would Mark live? Could this be the end?

Matthew Maley (11)
Marden High School, North Shields

Mission Chaos

She knew it was there but didn't want it to be. While the starvation was taking the best of her, she heard it. The screams outside haunted her and she could only hope that the screams wouldn't be her. Now they were getting louder.

"I'm here," a voice silently shrieked. She knew it was going to get her.

"Come here, little girl!" the voice said.

Her breathing got louder and the sound of footsteps got louder too. Again, the voice shrieked, "Come out, little girl. I won't hurt you."

But she knew it would. She wondered if she'd survive...

Charlotte Ainscow (11)

Marden High School, North Shields

Alien Invasion

Bang! War has commenced. Glancing frantically outside my window, I see a mysterious creature walking to my door. I can't make out what it is. *Crash!* The door has been kicked in. There is no time to lose. Citizens bellow for help. Jumping out of my window, I land on a wet creature. It's an alien.

While charging through the town of destruction, I hear people crying. Ninety percent of the hopeless citizens are now trapped.

Stumbling through the gloomy forest there is another explosion. Voices are crying in pain as they're chased by the aliens. It isn't the end.

Jonathan Maley (11)
Marden High School, North Shields

The World's Doom

In the future, within the city of Pripyat, radiation had stopped spewing and the city was habitable. One day, in the recently re-opened Chernobyl power plant, there was a rogue worker who had lost his mind, nobody knew. He disabled the coolant flow.

Hours later, the second disaster happened. People knew what had happened. They knew it was the end. Without a second thought, they rioted. They rebelled. They looted. Gangs fought, people were scared. Then it was over. The major meltdown happened. All reactors blew. Pripyat and its residents were no more. Ukraine was doomed because of radiation.

Haydon Piercy (11)
Marden High School, North Shields

The Fear

"Quickly, over here. They won't spot us."
We needed to get into the house and find the key to the roof so we could launch a counter-attack on the enemy. I'd heard the key was stored in the general's office, so we had to find it. I checked all the drawers in his desk. Suddenly, we heard footsteps.
"It's the general, hide," I whispered.
The general then shouted, "Who is that in my office?"
The general burst through the door and checked every centimetre of his room. We were shaking. Then suddenly, we were spotted by the general...

Rory Pattinson (11)
Marden High School, North Shields

Mission Chaos

The eerie air, the dark cloudy sky, the lava-covered floor. Alicia, Simon and Vikk all went to their local park. Simon said, "Let's go into the forest."
Alicia and Vikk weren't too sure about this but they did it anyway. Bombs, planes and fire were everywhere but little did they know, it was WWIII.
Vikk said, "We should start heading back."
Simon said, "It'll be fine!"
Bang! Bodies were everywhere. There were blood, guts and brains. They all ran to survive and say goodbye to their lives and the people they loved the most.

Cerys Carle (12)
Marden High School, North Shields

The Great Destruction

I picked my way through the rubble, gazing across the once placid landscape. Great crystals of ice blossomed in the nooks and crannies. I looked back at the small party, we were looking for survivors, the ones that could be trusted. I curled my hands around my thick grey horse. Another wave was coming, I could see the great clouds in the east.

"Halt," I called, seeing a smoky figure moving in the distance. "Mount and be careful, you know what happened to Lilly and Piptooth."

We slowly preceded to the tense figure, just hoping that this wasn't one.

Heather Marchbank (11)
Marden High School, North Shields

Chernobyl

Sirens flashed through the broken window. Shards of glass sat on the table of a garden shed. Miles away, disaster struck, reducing the Earth's population by four billion.

A man slowly opened his eyes. The hazy sky came apparent to him through a shattered roof. He grabbed the side of the table and lifted himself up. Radiation shrouded the atmosphere, breaking it up and shortening the oxygen supply. The man winced in pain as he glanced at his injury. He coughed and spluttered as he opened the wooden door and stepped out to see only destruction, mayhem and Chernobyl raging.

Dillon Stephen Burgess (11)
Marden High School, North Shields

Devils To Angels

"This is the end of some of the most memorable people in history," whispered the voices from Hell. "We don't deserve to be down here, though we may have killed them. They didn't deserve the spotlight."

Clambering out into the world in their ghostly bodies, they found themselves in the glorious place called Heaven. Their mission was now starting to become a reality. After hours of forcing the people in Heaven to kill the dead people in Hell, they eventually gave in and the innocent people in Heaven turned to devils and the devils into angels.

Jessica Hoolison (11)
Marden High School, North Shields

Trust No One

We were the only ones left. The zombie apocalypse had begun. I was in a group of my friends, fighting the world in a cabin with zombies surrounding us. They were breaking windows and smashing doors. We locked ourselves in the bathroom.
"I'm a goner. We're all goners!" Mike screamed.
I told John to load the shotgun but we were out of shells. I asked Jaccy about the flashlight to blind the zombies but the batteries were missing. I started panicking. My palms were sweaty and my heart beat faster. I emptied my pockets... Batteries *and* shells.

Jonny Rushent (11)
Marden High School, North Shields

Deep In The Dark

I was walking through the dark. I couldn't see anything. I heard screams behind me and I felt the hot fire against my face.

Suddenly, through all the screams, I heard a tiny whisper. "Come closer," it said. I didn't know what it was so I just ignored it. Then five seconds later, I heard it again. "Closer," it said. I ignored it again but then ten seconds went by and it said, "One little step."

I was looking everywhere but because it was so dark I couldn't see anything. I took one step forward. That was a big mistake...

Elizabeth Shannon (12)
Marden High School, North Shields

I Once Loved This City

My eyes were shrouded as I stared in disbelief. The city I once loved covered in red destruction, tearing down building after building. I rushed on, my legs pounding the ground. Then I heard it, "Down with the factory."

I knew the revolution had arrived. The air already black as I saw my city's nuclear plant burn to a crisp... *Bang!* A loud sound rattled my ears and radioactive debris scattered the landscape, leaving chaos and tyranny throughout my once lovely home. I couldn't look at it. I ran for my life. It was time for me to survive.

Rowan Bennett (11)
Marden High School, North Shields

Mission Chaos

Ever since the sixty-second war, the human race has struggled. Robots of death roam abandoned streets as people die to the virus. But all hope's lost for the gone and those immune as well. Every city has a secret. Yet nobody ever finds it. But the immunes, well that's a very different story.
Many years ago, those immune to the virus '103 Test' were ripped away from their families to be tested on. Now, it's chaos... Their brains manipulated and drained, they lie lifeless on the floor of what was once a city, a safe city. But then they came...

Harley Jay Leslie (11)
Marden High School, North Shields

House 13

It was 3am, two very close friends had one more house to knock on before going to their Halloween house. After knocking on the door, there was no answer. They knocked again and there was still no answer. As they slowly walked away, the cobwebbed door creaked open.

"Come and play with me," said a voice from inside. Slowly entering the house, all of the lights turned off.

"Help, help! Don't go inside, it's dangerous!" shouted the friends as they stumbled down the stairs. They recalled that the house was number thirteen...

Jack Shorting (11)
Marden High School, North Shields

The Gas Mask

There were whispers behind me but I couldn't make out what they said... I turned around slowly, expecting to see someone but nobody was there. Then another voice called from the direction I was looking but then I realised it wasn't whispering, it was a gas mask breathing. I could only see its head, no body or legs. Then the breathing got louder.

"Wait, I'm surrounded," I mumbled to myself. There were hundreds of floating gas masks of all different heights and sizes. Then I slowly drifted down, at least it felt like it, but I was dead.

Lewis Burton (11)
Marden High School, North Shields

Chemicals

Its been four days since the leak. The population is lowering rapidly. I'm trying to get used to the fact that I won't see my family again. It's all my fault. I was visiting the chemical plant with my family and I pressed the wrong button... Now they're gone. I still hear their faint screams in my head. It's painful to even think about it...

The emergency broadcast has just come through. The chemicals are in the sewers and the land, now it's not safe to drink water. We have already been told not to go outside. It's just chaos.

Alesha Assam (11)
Marden High School, North Shields

Destruction

It's boiling. Sweat ran down my face from the bombs and destruction around me. The people had gone rogue and there was no one to turn to. I was lost... Suddenly, I heard footsteps stomping closer to me. I shut my eyes, afraid of what I would see if I opened them. Then, I heard gunshots. *Bang!* I frantically fumbled around, looking for my gun, needing to fight back. I stood up, trying to open my eyes but I couldn't. Then I felt something speeding towards me... *Boom!* I was knocked off my feet and rapidly plummeted into the darkness...

Amara Jessica Rawlings (11)
Marden High School, North Shields

Mission Chaos

I woke up, all I remembered was my parents screaming, "Save yourself.." and darkness shaded my mind. I looked around. All I could see was smoke, burnt-down buildings and no life, or so I thought...

A few seconds later, I saw a red flashing light in the distance. *What could that be?* I wondered. Just then, I heard some voices from where the light was coming from. I squinted my eyes. All I saw was a million 'human' outlines, I ran towards them. That was a big mistake. Metal clunked, it was the sound of machines... A robot army.

Libby Alice Shaw (11)
Marden High School, North Shields

Here's War

In the city bombs struck, the noise grew louder by the second. Storms were appearing over buildings. Everyone was frightened. Grenades were thrown, guns were fired and war had begun.

"Come here, darling," they shouted.

I was hiding, not wanting to move. Someone screamed. Who? I don't know. Everyone was running towards a building, the one in flames. The one burning crashed to the ground. No one was left, everyone was gone. Everywhere was silent. My head was spinning. I was lost, storms were approaching. I felt the ground shake.

Eisha Sikka (11)
Marden High School, North Shields

Hell

The worldwide hell, tornadoes ripping up houses and trees, like ripping up the grass, it made it look easy. People made bad choices like looting because they were confused, there had never been such a bad hurricane. Children hugged their parents with terror in their eyes. Meanwhile, I tried to keep my sister calm, tears trickling from her eyes. I felt my dream-like heart racing wildly. My mum and dad were trying not to panic but their faces were pale with fear. My dog was whimpering under my bed. All of a sudden, a tree smashed through the window...

Gabriel Knox (12)
Marden High School, North Shields

The Final Few Seconds

Sprinting towards the bunker, I tried to escape the meteor shower. I was the only person left in the city; will I survive?

Crash! A giant meteor just hit the city - or what was left of it. It crushed the final ruins of my home.

Crying, sitting in the corner of the bunker, suddenly I heard a voice come from outside. I murmured with tears streaming down my face, "Hello? Is anyone there?"

Suddenly, without warning, everything went black and I felt myself be put onto a stretcher and quickly taken out of the room. Where was I going?

Ruben Parnell (11)

Marden High School, North Shields

Cave Stone

There wasn't much left of the town. It took everything. Jasmine and Jack pondered, it was only them and a few others who had survived.

They saw an old woman on her rocking chair. She saw them and shouted, "In there!"

She pointed at the old mine, nobody had been down there for years. The kids went inside, there were bloody handprints on the walls. There stood a podium with a blue, shining crystal on it. A small plaque read: 'This is the key to all your problems'. Suddenly, the rocks fell, covering their way out...

Josie Elizabeth Bowmaker (11)
Marden High School, North Shields

Trapped

One moment I'm in my room, next I'm in a whole new world. I'm in a room, the light slowly closing its door on me. Suddenly a childish voice giggles in the far corner. "Having fun?" it whispers in a psychotic tone. "If you want, I'll help you escape." Dumbfounded, I selfishly agreed. Confidently, I straightened myself up and waited for instructions. Unsure of where to step, I cautiously stepped and fell. That's all I remembered before I woke up in my soft, warm bed. It was only a bad dream, or was it?

Hollie Lawson Mills (11)
Marden High School, North Shields

The Warning

I write to you from thirty years in the future. I send this letter to warn you.

In three months, a rage-filled asteroid will hit Earth on July 28th. There will be no signs but trust me, it will happen. Tell the government, tell the people. Say everything, anything to warn them. Over half of the human race will be eliminated and the survivors will wish for death. This is a hostile world now, the hunters are the hunted. Tell the world or know your deathly, horribly fates. The world will suffer if you don't act now. Tell everyone, beware!

Jennifer Stutt
Marden High School, North Shields

The Thing

I silently crept among the bushes, or what was left of them anyway. I continued creeping, trying not to get caught by the Thing, the living, walking nightmare. The crunchy autumn leaves blew around like butterflies. *Crunch*. I'd stood on a leaf. I jerked aside, snapping a twig. I'd made far too much noise. A dark figure loomed over me, I stayed as still as I could. I don't think it mattered though, it came closer and closer until... I screamed. But I couldn't run for fear, my feet had left the ground. It'd caught me.

Molly Ballard (11)
Marden High School, North Shields

Save The World

On the 4th of July, America bombed North Korea. In response, Kim Jong-un launched the most dangerous nuke in the world. That nuke had a dangerous chemical that created a virus which would turn the human race into zombies. A group of survivors assembled to try to eliminate the virus by growing their own food and looting everything they saw.

One day, the zombies attacked the survivors in their sleep. So the survivors tried to defeat the virus but most of the survivors died. There was only one man left... It was him versus the last zombie...

Rory O'Neill (12)
Marden High School, North Shields

Mission Fallout

I could feel the heat on the back of his neck. I could see the explosion behind him. A nuclear war had begun...

I woke up. It's been three years since the war, gangs rule the streets and zombies roam in the wastelands. The Strauss gang are constantly on my back, demanding money. They could do anything they wanted, the authorities are dead. I have to sleep with a Magnum next to me, in case a zombie comes in. The world has fallen and there's nothing I can do about it.

Bang! Zombies are outside. I load my gun, ready...

Luke Brown (11)
Marden High School, North Shields

Eruption

As fast as I could, I sprinted towards the hideout, the volcano was about to erupt. To my right, I squinted through the humid, steamy air and saw a figure with its hands up. It was holding a camera. He was a man.

"Aargh!" he screamed. I recognised that voice from a mile away. The figure was Peter Parker. The floor vibrated. I was worrying, worrying a lot! The volcano erupted, what was Peter Parker going to do? His webs couldn't attach to the lava. He couldn't be saved. He had fallen and he was rolling. Was he okay? No.

Harry James Wallace (12)
Marden High School, North Shields

The End Of The Glorious World

It happened. It was bad. It was the worst possible thing that could ever happen in the history of life. Everything happened so quick and fast. Buildings were shambles, cars were ripped open and pavements and roads were cracked with fury. There were bodies washed up on the shore. People were on the high ground desperate to not be destroyed, but there was a part of them inside that was broken and filled with misery. Nothing could help or encourage them to do more. It was like all their happiness was ripped apart by this event. It was the end.

Samuel Rushent (11)
Marden High School, North Shields

Mission Chaos

I sprinted towards the bunker as bombs dropped behind me, echoing the horrifying sounds of screams so loud but yet so silent. I entered the bunker and ferociously slammed the door behind me. It wasn't long before I realised I wasn't alone. "Follow me," whispered something, emerging in the darkness around me. "Another step, keep going." Something took over me, I listened, taking the step. I tried to resist it but it was so strong that I couldn't stop. Every step I took, the more powerful it was...

Jayda Kershaw (11)
Marden High School, North Shields

The Hurricane

It was a stormy night when an unusual feeling was in everyone's heads. When it was pitch-black in the morning, a hurricane hit right in the centre of the city. The whole city was destroyed, so to live, people started fighting for food and people were killing one another. People started becoming zombies and poisoning the rest of the city. The end was near for humans, there was one left. He couldn't go into the city because it had been raided by zombies until night time. The zombies found him and backed him into a ledge, he fell...

Taylor Walker (11)
Marden High School, North Shields

The Terrible Zombie Apocalypse

It all happened in just two days, in 2017. A zombie apocalypse targeted another person. He was called Bruno. This had happened to his dad, he didn't make it out alive. It was basically impossible. Bruno was trying his best to get away but he ran out of water and food, it was over thirty degrees and there was no getting out. Bruno just lay down and gave up. The apocalypse took over the city and eliminated the population. It was all devastating. There was so much damage. The horrible thought was that over two thousand people had died.

Tom George Warne (11)
Marden High School, North Shields

The Meteor

All of sudden, a gigantic meteor could be seen, it was going to crash on the Earth. The meteor crashed down, it was like a huge explosion. Nearly every person on Earth died but the people who did survive, they knew that they weren't going to survive for long. There was no shelter that they could find and they couldn't find any food. They knew they were going to die and they were people who had survived the meteor. They were panicking. It was chaos but as days went by, they started dying and there wasn't a living thing alive.

Malachi Taylor (11)
Marden High School, North Shields

Captured By Nightfall

As the electrifying storm captured the world, he slowly crept through the deserted forest, desperate to return home. Suddenly, a cool, crisp wind went gushing past his face sending a spine-chilling sensation running through his body.

"Come with me," a dangerous voice whispered. Following the voice deeper into the forest, he came face-to-face with an abandoned mansion and cautiously entered. As glass shattered from the ceiling, a huge hand captured his shoulder and dragged him to the ground. He was never seen again.

Macey McKean (11)
Marden High School, North Shields

Mission Chaos

"Drink it!" whispered what sounded like a zombie. I was shaking, not knowing what to do. Should I drink it?

"Just drink it..." the voice said again.

I took a tiny sip of the drink that looked like rotten milk. After I drank some, I couldn't feel my hands.

"Drink more," the voice whispered again. I drank more. Suddenly, I couldn't feel my arms.

"Drink it all."

I drank it all. My legs started to hurt. I fell to the ground. What should I do? Should I call for help?

Philippa Springle (11)
Marden High School, North Shields

War's End

"Follow me, Private," my sergeant shouted. The tank shook as it drove over bits of debris. "Incoming!"

An artillery shell struck the building to the left of us. I fell off the tank and cut my leg. I couldn't get up and lost consciousness.

When I woke up, I lifted the bricks off my body and stood up. I bandaged up the wound and picked up my rifle. Everything was different. The sky was red, everything was on fire and I couldn't find my squad. I limped down the street and realised we had lost.

Thomas Armstrong (11)
Marden High School, North Shields

Plastic Damage

"I found something," she shouted.

I prowled towards the animal, hoping it was the best thing ever.

"But it's dead!" I sighed sadly, the turtle was lying on the ground. Its tummy was cut open with plastic pouring out.

"That was our only food until we humans destroyed it," I said with sorrow.

I knew that it was our fault. We used single-use plastic and the animals died. That was the last animal in the world. Now it's just my friend and me, the only living things in the world.

Francesca Herzberg (11)
Marden High School, North Shields

Mental War

I drifted off into deep sleep, my brain shutting down. This wasn't my normal bed. I was taken to the park with my kind and caring mum. She was playing hide-and-seek with me. The other children often played among the tall pines just off by the fence. Then the dreaded missile hit. It was so unexpected. There wasn't a war going on, that I'd heard of... Then more hit. Bodies were flying everywhere, somehow I didn't get hurt because I was in a tunnel.

Then I woke up, my parents came in and said we had to evacuate.

Andrew Joseph Scott (11)
Marden High School, North Shields

Animal Invasion!

In the jungle lived a lot of animals, they loved the forest very much. One day, all the animals had to say goodbye to the forest and hello to a zoo. The animals hated it at the zoo, *hated* it. Then Lion had an idea to take over the world.

A couple of days later, that's what happened. Everyone was bowing to him. All the animals were using humans as slaves. Lion thought he had everyone under his control but then he heard footsteps. He turned and saw a big, mighty man who said, laughing, "Not everyone."

Alexis Jane Elliott (11)
Marden High School, North Shields

The Water

The screams outside fell silent. The day had come.
Gallons of water flushed through the town, over
houses and swinging branches of trees. *Is this the
end?* The devastation spread further and further.
Dirty water leaked under doorways filling up to
footsteps to ground floors. Precious memories
washed away along with hopeful people.
Weeks and weeks of cleaning up to be done, slowly
became longer and longer. But something wasn't
right, nobody was around to help. Families were
left alone, fighting for their lives.

Lily Rose Hobkirk (11)
Marden High School, North Shields

Chaos

A bright light burst from the horizon. Jack ran towards it to see what it was. It was a helicopter. It must have crashed. When Jack peeked inside he was shocked to see his poor grandad, blood gushing out of him. When Jack asked him if he was okay, he didn't answer. Jack realised he wasn't alive anymore. Jack poured out with tears.
A nuke landed and the air wasn't safe to breathe, he passed out because of the lack of air.
When he woke up, he was in the bunker with his friends and family surrounding him...

Charlie David Gilchrist (11)
Marden High School, North Shields

We Lost

We were the only ones left. Darkness filled our bodies. Pain scattered across our worthless hearts. "Come," a voice whispered.

Where did it come from? Silently, I tiptoed to what I thought was the end of my hopeless life. A cold, wet and bloodied knife vanished into my stomach. I was dead. Darkness now turned cold as blood shot out of my stomach. This was the end. This was the end. This was the end. Now my life couldn't walk the happy life I could've died for. I was trapped, I was dead for life.

Chloe Hadland (10)

Marden High School, North Shields

Mission Chaos

The nuke hit yesterday. I was lucky enough to survive the blast but zombies are everywhere. I'm on a floating platform but we need more fuel and it's located on the other side of the canyon. The problem is, how do I get back? If I don't, I'll be lunch. Wait, if I blow up a canister, I'll be launched up so I can get home.

Bang! The canister exploded and I'm now gliding back to the platform. Touchdown! I'm going to fill it up now, that's for a week. I'll have to go back soon.

Jake Waddell (11)
Marden High School, North Shields

Mission Chaos

I was surrounded by bombs exploding and children screaming. I was alone, I didn't know where Lily, Mum or Dad had gone.

"You! Come here," it whispered.

Suddenly, a bomb exploded right next to me but there was a girl who was standing in front of me. I thought I was just seeing things but I blinked a few times and she was still there. I asked her what her name was but I heard an explosion which was so loud I couldn't hear what she said. I asked her again and I looked behind me. Then she was gone.

Olivia Taylor Appleby (11)
Marden High School, North Shields

The Big Bang!

A bright light burst out from the horizon. It was the first day of the war. I saw all of the machines marching into the fields ahead. *Bang!* The first bomb had been launched. *Bang!* Blood splattered me and all of my group. Suddenly, I saw a bomb coming towards me. I ran but my friend got hit by it. I carried on running, then I got shot. Someone spotted me and picked me up, sprinting towards the bunker. He made it. I was safe.

The weeks passed slowly. Then suddenly, the screams outside fell silent...

Freya Elizabeth Yare (11)

Marden High School, North Shields

Disaster Strikes

The machine guns rattled my brain. It sent shivers down my spine. I stayed sheltered in the bunker. Bombs blew up the entire war ground. My heart was pounding out my chest. I could hear the squadron leader barking orders. It all blurred out, my mind was whirring. I knew my name was being called but I didn't at the same time. My brain felt lost, why wasn't I pursuing the orders? I felt weary - this was too much to handle. My life had been flipped upside down and I wasn't sure if I was ready to face it...

Isla Hodgson (11)
Marden High School, North Shields

The End In Darkness

I trembled. The end was near.

"Hurry up, " whispered a voice as another one screamed. Where were they coming from? Darkness covered Earth like a blanket.

"We need to be quick," a mysterious voice said.

I squinted my eyes, staring hard to try and make out a face. Unfortunately, I had no luck. As the world became silent, I could feel my spine shivering. Footsteps. I could hear footsteps. I followed the sound of the footsteps. Then I found the earth was no longer beneath my feet...

Emmeline Law (11)
Marden High School, North Shields

The End Of The World

I heard a huge explosion. Everything went into complete darkness.

When I woke up, the world looked miserable, buildings turned to ash, water had evaporated. The world was a desert. This was when I knew I was the last one left. I heard the ground shake, then I felt it. I fell over onto the ground and a huge piece of the Earth's core tore out of the ground. It came towards me. I ran as fast as I could to the shelter but I couldn't. It came for my head and then I heard myself say, "It was me."

Thomas Dennis Russell (11)
Marden High School, North Shields

Disastrous Earth

I fell down to my knees, my crimson-red blood pouring... A monster of swirling wind followed me as I ran, already my heart was racing. I tripped up on my own emotion to see flaming rocks hit our disastrous Earth, causing major vibrations to the already broken ground. I got up, running so fast I couldn't feel my pain, my sorrow. I stopped for some stupid reason, I stopped. Just for a second, I stopped. Now the pain was getting to me. I fell to my knees, exhaling my crimson blood. I could hardly breathe.

Lucas Bell (11)

Marden High School, North Shields

Pandemonium

I suddenly regained consciousness. I tried to pick myself up but my foot was stuck. I sat down for a second and heard a small hiss and realised it was a gas leak. I had to get out of there before I was blown to smithereens. I lifted the rubble off my foot and ran. I ran and ducked behind a small hut. I peeked around it, seconds later there was an enormous bang. Instantly, groups of men rushed out of houses with guns and weapons. They opened fire at each other, it was pandemonium. Then someone shot me.

Joseph McAvelia (11)
Marden High School, North Shields

Missing Then Murdered

This was his first camping trip and maybe his last. There was a six-year-old boy named Noah. He was so excited as he was going on a family camping trip in the middle of a forest in Whitby. When he arrived, it was late at night, so they set their tents up and went straight to bed.

Once dawn arrived, his family soon realised that their brother and son were missing. After twenty-four hours, they rang the police.

As days turned into weeks, the police eventually found the poor boy. He was dead!

Erin Leanne Goicoechea (11)
Marden High School, North Shields

Destruction Of The Fire

There was thunder and lightning in the centre of the city. It was all quiet until a violent man caused more destruction with fire. I could hear the sirens coming to help. I saw the gang, who looked like teenagers, getting away. I called 999 for the police. Then I chased after them. Running out of breath, my chest pumping like a lion roaring, I still carried on. The fire got bigger. The firemen weren't helping at all. I stopped for a couple of seconds but when I looked up, there was no one there.

Connie Yeomans (11)
Marden High School, North Shields

Apart From Me

It was coming closer, the giant thunderstorm was coming closer! The sky turned grey and everyone was rushing out of their homes trying to find help. Suddenly, it went quiet and then lightning struck. The noise was deafening considering it hit my neighbour's house.

I woke up twelve hours later in a demolished hospital with nobody around.

"Hello?" I shouted, but I heard no reply. Then I looked out the window to find out that everyone apart from me had been killed by the fire.

Lilly Hunter (11)
Marden High School, North Shields

World War One

He did it. My brother's time machine worked and he brought us to World War One. I took a cautious step away from him. Looking down, I saw the endless pile of dead bodies and the sand which was ruined by the blood that once belonged to the patriotic soldiers.

All of a sudden, there was a bang. I looked at my brother, who was hit by the bullet. I couldn't bear to look at him as he was dying. Tears ran down my face as I saw another bullet. It was a bullet that was directly aimed at me...

William Ridsdale (11)
Marden High School, North Shields

Eternal Darkness

I fell. A deafening screech tore at my ears. His scarred, torn face looked fearless in the chaos around. The empire was destroyed, I was lost, the end was near. I saw the cold, dark bodies lying in the midst of death. The castle crumbling, the village burning. All was lost. They had won, fire spat at me as I moved away, ready to run. All of a sudden, out the corner of my eyes, I saw a crossbow on the bloodied corpse of a warrior. He was there in front of me. I shot and the pointed arrow struck.

Ryan Nolan (11)
Marden High School, North Shields

The Outbreak

In a city called Coin City, it was peaceful and calm until the chaos broke out. There was a nuke and not many survived. I was able to get in my bunker but many didn't just die, they turned into zombies! I walked outside, covering my eyes. I haven't seen the sun in years. Then a zombie grabbed my back and I turned around, punching it in the face. The mushy flesh covered my fist and then it died. I know I won't last over a month in this place. This is war, this is Mission Chaos!

Finley Taylor (11)
Marden High School, North Shields

The End

The town was dead, no one was there. It was empty. The sun scorched the Earth. There was drought and famine. I was abandoned, left in an old garage. I had no choice but to find food. I started to forage for two hours but nothing. Finally, I saw an old corner shop and it was fully stocked. I started toward it. Suddenly, there was a loud bang followed by darkness. I tried to ease my way out but something grabbed me and dragged me back. I kicked and pulled. Suddenly, lights turned on and silence.

Daniel Robert Grieveson (11)

Marden High School, North Shields

Story Of Element 115

It was a stormy day. I was afraid. I was in the jungle when suddenly I found three people chatting about a zombie apocalypse. I approached them and they told me how the outbreak happened. It was a doctor who had tried to rule the world with element 115 which was locked in Japan. They were trying to destroy it because it was the source of the zombies. I asked if I could help and they agreed. So we hatched a plot. Suddenly, we heard the zombies. Luckily, we were armed, it was time to kill.

Adyan Ahmed (11)
Marden High School, North Shields

Zombie

It started as a boiling hot day in the jungle. Suddenly clouds blew over and it started to thunder like crazy. A giant spaceship came crashing out of the clouds. Zombies came dropping out of the spaceship.

All I heard were screams for help. I went to the city to have a look. No one was there. I walked a little bit further and looked to my left, a zombie looked at me. It shouted at me and all of a sudden, it started chasing me. I tripped over. It came and ate me alive. The city was over.

Joseph Gilmour (11)
Marden High School, North Shields

The Fire

Darkness shrouded the land. I didn't know where I was going or where I was. The aroma of smoke filled the air. My eyes were adjusting to the darkness and I could see the clouds caving in above me. Then the roaring thunder came crashing down and the rain covered the land. I went from a fast walk to a run. I was running to safety but I couldn't see anything or anybody. Then, out in the distance, I saw a light. I ran only to find out that the light was fire and that fire was my death.

Eve Thomas (11)

Marden High School, North Shields

Unrest

I was inside my living room when the TV showed *Breaking News*. It said the government had been shut down and that the fight to the death had begun... I heard people setting fires and shooting guns. That was then but now, it was worse. If I walk on the streets, I see dead bodies and I could get killed by a gang. Toxic diseases have spread, underground hospitals were destroyed and doctors burnt to death. In this world, you kill or be killed. No truth, no rules and nowhere to hide.

Isabelle Hannant (11)
Marden High School, North Shields

World Of Hell

The world was changing, we had to adapt. Smoke and gas choked the world like a cloak of hell and torment. It had begun. The screams of dying people rattled through the air but were silenced by gunshots. As darkness crept over us, everything tensed because this night could be the end of our lives in this dead world. My mind was whirring as I took one tentative step forward. I wanted to go back but if I did I knew I would be killed. Cautiously, I took one more step. A gun fired. I fell.

Matthew Aust (11)

Marden High School, North Shields

War Wrecks

In the catastrophic, disastrous period of revolution and war, dawn until dusk battles rage and tear apart the world. As the uncontrollable catastrophes occur throughout the globe, the inevitable truth is that every day the atmosphere is damaged and will at one point, never emit light again. Lightning roars. People scream. Light fades. In the closing day of the human race, life is being erased as the overthrown, broken government desperately attempts to support. Will they ever stop?

Alexander Slaven (11)
Marden High School, North Shields

The Zombie Apocalypse

We were the only ones left. It was March 10th when the outbreak happened. My crew and I were in the abandoned mall. We had a plan to board up the food shop for the night and attempt to find help the next day. Of course, I was on night watch. In the dead of night, I heard a huge bang. I looked out and saw a horde of them, the zombies. I panicked as they came flocking in. I tried to call for help but no one came. Suddenly, the zombies were getting closer but it was too late...

Jack Wardlaw (11)
Marden High School, North Shields

The Cave

I was running, running from robotic zombies. Darkness covered the land. I felt a sudden drop and fell down onto my knees. My mind drifted off into nothing.

A couple of minutes later, I woke and stood up. A few seconds later, a hissing noise came to my ears. I slowly turned around only to see giant metal cave spiders. I had to turn but someone had warned me that if I made any sudden moves when they were looking at me, they'd pounce. I tried it and they pounced on me...

Aaron Karaboga (11)

Marden High School, North Shields

Humans' End

One day, a boy was in a cave and he walked deep into it and found a shiny stone. It was blue like the sky. He got it out of the wall and he heard a scream, it was horrifying. He dropped the stone and it made a whooshing noise. Then a portal opened and thousands of dragons came out. Then the power went out. Everything went dark as a huge dragon came out and destroyed the world, making Earth its nest. So all the humans were never seen again. The human race was finally over.

Jack
Marden High School, North Shields

The Dark

As a metal lamp fell, I didn't know how to get out of my house. The door was locked. I had no way of getting out. *Bang!* I heard a sound from the kitchen, I walked in. I saw a smashed plate on the floor. I heard knocking on the door. The door creaked open. I hid behind the sofa and I heard a lot of screaming along the street. I was worried. I saw a shadow but it wasn't a human. It was a ghost. I saw blood all over the floor, I was worried and was afraid.

Jack Sutherland (11)
Marden High School, North Shields

Mission Chaos

I woke up in a strange environment. I was wondering where I was, looking about curiously. I heard a noise coming from outside, it sounded like screaming but I was too scared to leave the bunker. It was getting annoying now. I checked what was going on and I silently opened the door. Stood in front of me were some creatures and for some reason, I think they wanted me dead. I ran for my life but there were more, there was a swarm of them around me. What should I do?

Malaika Souza (11)
Marden High School, North Shields

That One Zombie

One blood-curdling night, Piper set off out into the woods, crunching every twig that came upon her tracks. The screams outside fell silent and she knew she wasn't safe. Swiftly, she turned her head and found herself staring at five brain-eating zombies, slowly walking towards her. They had marched, the war had begun.

"Two steps forward," the voice in her head whispered.

She did as they said and she was plunged into complete darkness...

Holly Howells (11)
Marden High School, North Shields

The Water

I could hear screams echoing in the world outside. As water levels rose across from the dead, homes were destroyed and lives were at risk. Questions roared through my mind. *Is this the end? What should I do? Will this ever end?* I could see the terror on people's faces as their lives receded. "Is anyone in there?" shouted an unknown voice. However, I shouted and yelled but no one heard me. The water was too strong and powerful.

Molly Dowse (11)

Marden High School, North Shields

Bomb At The Sun

It's been seventy days. Every day, the sun looks smaller. That's what happens when a bunch of humans send a huge bomb towards the sun. They practically blew it up. As the sun gets smaller, the sky gets darker. With no sun to help us, humanity probably won't survive for much longer. Each day, somebody vanishes. I hope that tomorrow's victim won't be me. However, as the sun helps us so much, I don't think anyone will survive much longer.

Emma Melvin (11)
Marden High School, North Shields

Asteroid Invasion

Raining terror. Red smoke filled my view of the area around me as one by one, hundreds of asteroids smacked down destructively on the Earth's face. I was stuck on a deserted island with my foot trapped under a heavy grey stone, I couldn't escape. It was like being in a microwave as temperatures started to rise dramatically. The ground began to shake as the island began to sink into the bottomless, ice-cold water. I would never see daylight again...

Olivia May Chaplow (11)

Marden High School, North Shields

War Of Hell

As I ran towards the gate which was wide open, gunshots whistled over my head as the Germans tried to stop me. I just ran faster and faster. In the distance, I could see the train I had arrived on five months ago. I don't know why they took me away, because my dad had put his coat with the Star of David on it. He was a Jew, but I wasn't. So when they took me away, I tried to tell them I wasn't a Jew, but they still took me away from my family.

Sandy Bainton (11)
Marden High School, North Shields

Mission Chaos

Darkness fell and lightning struck, children were terrified. *Knock, knock, knock.* Everyone screamed. One child checked who it was and passed out. A little voice which sounded very creepy said, "I have sweets for you, just open the door."
As three children went to open the door, there was nothing but dripping blood from the windows.
Then five killer clowns stepped inside and all they could hear was screaming and choking.

Preben Koldal (11)
Marden High School, North Shields

The End?

Is this the end? Is this the moment which is yet to arrive? The TV showed us the future but it was useless. It all hit me like a heavy raindrop. The anger inside me raged before everyone. Why though? We helped the Earth as much as we could, so why was our outcome this? I was totally perplexed. *Global warming: Please be aware!* I had too many emotions, I just couldn't express it all. A cold knife just cut the atmosphere.

Ankitha Ramesh (11)
Marden High School, North Shields

The End

A man called John woke up one day and it was a normal day. As he looked out of the window, like he did every day, everything was gone. All of a sudden, the world went black, at this point, his heart started racing faster than it had ever raced before. His heart then stopped. John's house was the only one standing. Questions went through his mind. *Where is everyone? What's happened?* He thought it was the end of his life.

Emma Jammeh (11)
Marden High School, North Shields

Mission Chaos

I lie here, wondering what went wrong. How I created so much destruction. It seems the end goal is getting further and further away each day. *Our world is never going to the same*, I thought to myself. *Why did I try and bring new technology when it wasn't ready to be used?* I don't know what I should do. Flames surround me, making Earth another sun. Are we going to have to move to the moon or maybe Mars?

Nathan Potts (11)
Marden High School, North Shields

Snapped

I squinted at the red smoke through the glass. A large figure glowed red in the cracks as the symbol flashed, *My Mind Bleeds.* All the objects broke. The figure disappeared. Then, as I sniffed the air, I was blasted into the open. All of my limbs snapped quickly before I was thrown up into the dark sky. I smashed in half and then in half again. All I felt was sorrow. Then the figure snapped its claws and disappeared.

Zachary Cook (10)
Marden High School, North Shields

Help!

"Help!" it whispered. I suddenly stopped and looked around but there was no one there.
"Closer," it said again, so I moved closer and closer. There I fell into a dark black hole.
The voice said, "Come closer."
I stopped and didn't move an inch closer because there was something there.
"Help!" I screamed with all my might, but no one could hear me.

Chloe Shanks (11)
Marden High School, North Shields

Zombie City

Conner sprinted. Zombies were everywhere, there was no place to hide, nowhere to go. After Connor jumped over a few bodies and ran into a building, he crouched behind a till as he heard people screaming. The human population was decreasing. After looking around the building, he found a pistol. Connor smashed the window on the second floor. He was aiming at their zombie heads, slowly killing them one by one.

Thomas Ratcliffe (11)
Marden High School, North Shields

The Day Of The End!

I was the only one left, all of my friends carried on without me. All was lost. Nowhere to go, I was completely lost in the middle of the jungle. I knew where to find water.

Soon, I came to an abandoned stream. I scooped up some water and began to drink. All of a sudden, there was a stripy tiger beside me. I was stuck... What could I do? I kept staring into its eyes until it pounced. I was doomed.

Esme Robb (11)
Marden High School, North Shields

Fall

A twenty-year-old man called Paul was walking down the street. Suddenly he started to hear a whistling sound and looked around to see the source of the noise. Paul looked up to see the moon plummetting to the ground. Paul screamed, "Look!" as he saw the moon getting bigger and bigger and bigger. All he could hear were screams filling the air. All went silent as he heard the loudest bang ever.

Oscar George Richardson (11)
Marden High School, North Shields

The Fire

It was a dark, misty night during winter. Anne was clearing her mind from the day she'd had when all of a sudden, she heard a spark crackling. Scared, she called her boyfriend Phillip and she told him to put the fire out immediately.

As he rushed to her rescue, the fire became more severe. By the night, the smoke swirled around the forest like a tornado as they evacuated and rushed to safety.

Gracie Pears (11)
Marden High School, North Shields

Darkness

Sophie was walking down her street. She was just minding her own business when she suddenly heard a noise, it sounded like thunder. She looked up. The sky was changing colour, it was changing into different colours. The noise was drawing her in. She drew closer and closer and closer. She felt the urge to go closer. Then she looked down and if she took one more step, she would fall into the darkness...

Erin McEntee (11)
Marden High School, North Shields

Pandemonium

This is it, *will I survive?* Bottles crash against the buildings and against the cars as I battle the riots. They bomb me and shoot me as smoke fills the air. I say to myself that I'll survive as a bullet suddenly hits me.

I wake up and I think, *where am I?* I'm in a hospital bed fighting for my life. Tubes in my heart, wearing a mask for clean air... I die.

Will Jones (11)
Marden High School, North Shields

The Unending War

The sky grew dark, everything went by in a blur. The helpless screams rang in our ears for days. We all staggered forward in the hope that this would change everything. The heavy snow lay down on the battlefield, the poppies now crystalised with ice. The war had begun. Guns firing. Fires blazing. Bodies lay on the muddy terrain. Many of these people were unaware that this was their end.

Jasmine Lily Lee (11)
Marden High School, North Shields

Bang!

I looked outside and saw a blinding light. My eyes couldn't help but follow this light and my legs just moved with them. I stepped outside, still attached to this shine. I suddenly felt cold air beneath me, I noticed I was falling. Out of the blue, it felt like I'd stopped falling and had landed in sticky liquid. I heard footsteps coming closer and closer. Then I heard a bang...

Hajar Al-Sabbahy (11)
Marden High School, North Shields

Game Over

The terrible beast slowly made its way towards me, devouring everything in sight. Then I realised, I would be next. I ran as fast as my legs would carry me. It ate all the trees in the world and drank all the water. No trees meant no oxygen. No water meant no one would survive. It would be the end of the human race. The world would be over in a matter of days. It would be pure darkness.

Libby Bilcliffe (11)
Marden High School, North Shields

Fireballs In The Sky

I looked up into the sky and was shocked. The sky wasn't blue anymore, it was a strange shade of green. There was also a gargantuan fireball heading straight towards me. Suddenly, there wasn't just one fireball, there were hundreds heading straight towards me. I kept hearing lots of bangs and people screaming. Just then, a fireball hit me but I wasn't anywhere near ready.

Olivia Watson (11)

Marden High School, North Shields

World War Zombie

It all started when it thundered and everyone turned into a zombie except for me. *How did this happen?* I thought to myself. I knew I had to survive. After a while of hiding from the zombies, one of them came closer with a gun. *Where could I run?* They had surrounded the town like a fence. I stepped back, not knowing what was there but luckily, there was nothing.

Liam Skipsey (11)
Marden High School, North Shields

Darkness

My head was spinning. My ears were ringing. I couldn't tell if I was in a nightmare or reality. All of a sudden, I felt my legs move... I wasn't using them. A voice called, "Take a step forward... Go on."
I did.
"Take another one."
I did, every step felt easier and easier. I took one more step and fell into the jaws of darkness.

Jonathan Lawson Mills (11)
Marden High School, North Shields

Sun-Drained

Early one Wednesday morning, several people walked the streets of the colossal city, cars drifting by. A man by the name of Joseph looked up to admire the warm weather when suddenly, he couldn't look away. Large empires of alien ships fired large beams of water into the sun. He was confused until suddenly, it went very bright and then... total darkness.

William Clarkson (11)
Marden High School, North Shields

The War Of The World

I am writing this in case the world ends tomorrow. Today the sun just disintegrated and there has been drought everywhere. The main leaders of the world were assassinated. Yesterday, there were no more laws. The world is corrupting and I am in the middle of it. Now, as there are no laws, people are looting houses. This truth is the end of the world.

Tilly Smith (11)
Marden High School, North Shields

The Final Day

Loading my rifle, getting ready to pull the trigger, I knew this would be my last chance to take the victory of this deadly war. *Bang!* The first shot rippled across the isolated city, sending hundreds more off. As explosions were sent off, I didn't know what would be coming my way. Another day to live or not much longer for my heart to beat?

Harry Jacob Short (11)
Marden High School, North Shields

Lost...

We were the only ones left. I sprinted towards the bunker and instantly fell silent. If only I'd been just as quick as a flash. My friend and I looked around the bloodied walls and saw innocent children looking deep into my soul. They said, "He's coming for you."
After that, I turned to my friend and said, "Run!"

Hayden Dunning (11)
Marden High School, North Shields

The Four Men

Everything was ablaze. Thousands of people flooded the streets as buildings fell rapidly behind them; their deafening screams drowned out in the gunfire. When the smoke cleared, four men emerged from the wreckage. They were dressed head to toe in camo and held rifles. As I ran out of my car and headed for safety, we made eye contact...

Ava Lauren Taylor (11)
Marden High School, North Shields

Mission Chaos

It was as if the world had ended... As my eyes slowly awoke, all surroundings were unclear. Barely being able to stand up, I limped around, only to notice that nobody was able to be seen. Curious yet startled, confused and petrified, it was as if I was the only one here... The last girl standing. The ground shook. The wind squealed!

Isla Russell (11)
Marden High School, North Shields

Darkness Had Fallen

She thought it'd be a typical day. She woke up, not knowing that war was approaching. Darkness had fallen and the next thing she heard was the deathly siren, indicating war was about to commence. What could she possibly do? Racing to her front door, her heart dropped as she realised that she was alone. It was the end.

Ella McKean (11)

Marden High School, North Shields

The End

The room was full of survivors and there was a deadly silence within it. Three loud knocks broke the silence. Everyone stared at the door.

At that moment, all the lights began to flicker and wails flooded the room. Everything stopped. Blood painted the walls and bodies were hanging from the ceiling.

Luke Robert Potts (11)

Marden High School, North Shields

Zombie Chaos

Suddenly, I saw something, it was coming from the sky. It looked like a meteor, it was coming from the sky faster than a cheetah. The meteor hit an old, abandoned house in the woods.

When I ran towards the house, I saw loads of zombies. I picked up a pickaxe and chopped the zombies' heads off.

Jamie Dunn (12)

Marden High School, North Shields

Mission Chaos

A bright light appeared from the horizon. People stared at the glimmering light. Dark figurines appeared from on top of the mountain that slightly covered the sun.

Civilians rushed towards the hidden bunker that was underneath the sausage shop. But one man stared as zombies rushed into the town...

Charlie Chambers (11)
Marden High School, North Shields

Biological Chaos

"Get down," yelled a voice in the distance but Tom just kept running. *Bang!* A scream! The army came out from where they were hiding and suddenly, out of nowhere, came Tom. Alive, bloodied, but alive. With a sweep of his torch, they all burst into flames.

Jack Harker (11)
Marden High School, North Shields

War

Guns were firing, people were dropping to the floor, but there was one man called Tyler. He was the main man. He took down planes, people and tanks. It was two versus 1,100. Bodies began dropping like stones. The 1,100 were dead at a hundred a minute!

Cameron Alexander Ross (11)

Marden High School, North Shields

The Light

A bright light burst from the horizon. Screams echoed in the tightly packed room. Babies, women and young children cried - gushing with blood. "You're the last known survivors. It's up to you to protect the Earth," yelled someone over the speakers. Us men were rushed out of the large, cramped room. We made it. The creatures had taken over everything. *Slash! Thud!* I ran a strange weapon through the devil's chest. I kept on fighting. *Crash!* Bombs fell from the sky. Everything sounded muffled and high-pitched, like squeals. Suddenly, everything went black.

I woke up in my warm bed.

Mae Withrow (12)

Wyvern Academy, Eggleston View

The Screaming Dead

The screams outside fell silent. I was all alone. After the incident, all the lost were buried in Chester graveyard, beside my house. That day, strangely, some people cancelled their trips last minute because they thought something horrific would happen to that boat. They were right. Their screams pierced the watcher's ears as it left the dock. Trauma, unforgettable torture. I was there at the moment the boat sank. Horrific images flood my head daily. I've had a curse of hearing the dead since the incident occurred. They scream for help all day but I can't help them. I'm useless.

Faith Parry (12)
Wyvern Academy, Eggleston View

War Zone Reality

It'd finally arrived, my VR headset. After months of waiting, it was here. Without losing a second, I ran to get on the new game *War Zone Reality*.

I was in. Sprinting through the abandoned house, excitedly leaping downstairs, I tripped. The sensor jacket protected me somewhat but it actually hurt. Incredible!

Hours later, I'd found that the food actually worked, so I could play longer.

Days later. It was so repetitive, no gun upgrades or rematches. It was time to stop...

I wasn't in my room, it wasn't a game but reality, a war zone. I was a murderer!

Isaac Matthew Marlow (12)

Wyvern Academy, Eggleston View

The Hand

I sprinted towards the crooked bunker as the murky, heavy clouds carpeted the sky. Sweat dripped off my forehead and my hand gripped the freezing cold handle. Finally, I was safe. Just as I thought I was safe in the monstrosity, the screams fell silent. The machines marched, the war had begun.

"Come with me," a mysterious voice whispered. My head whipped around faster than lightning to search for the suspicious sound. Darkness filled the bunker and a skinny, crippled hand grabbed mine. "Argh!"

I was gone. I didn't know why or where to... Was this over?

Connie Ward (14)
Wyvern Academy, Eggleston View

The Day

Normal day, normal town. No one expects anything out of the usual to happen; today that would change. Walking home, the tension hangs in the air. A sudden change in atmosphere, people, strangers drop to their knees one by one, clutching their throat. I hold my breath, half-scared, half-aware. They start turning a subtle shade of blue before suddenly gasping. You can see the lungs inflate from behind their chest. A sudden, inhuman, pain-filled scream fills the once-tense air. An immense bang fills the air before utter silence. A vibration graces the air. I turn. Rubble everywhere.

Libby Graham (12)
Wyvern Academy, Eggleston View

The Black Death

"Just breathe..." I whispered, crawling through the dusty air vent in the abnormal, abandoned mansion. My leg was trapped in the floor of the disgusting vent. I screamed in agony as my skin ripped off my leg, squirting blood around like a water fountain. Pulling my useless body across the floor, I tried to escape my worst nightmare. The air vent cluttered as a demon-like black figure appeared and crawled towards me like a lion hunting its prey.

A giant gust of wind barged through as the black figure approached me and screamed, "You must now die!"

Joshua Baker (13)
Wyvern Academy, Eggleston View

Charlie

The street was dark and misty, black wheelie bins were in sight. Suddenly, a large group of boys arose from the darkness, closing in on Charlie. They pounced. *Bang!* It went black as the murder of crows drew nearer and nearer.
When Charlie awoke, a slinging pain shot throughout his whole body. The street was light now.
As Charlie realised the time, he sprinted to school unusually fast. As Charlie got into school it was already break time. Since Charlie was getting weird stares, he decided to go to the bathroom. That's when he saw it...

Amber Grace Matthews (13)
Wyvern Academy, Eggleston View

Last Glimpse Of Aspiration

Crops and water supply were a slim expense. Cattle and farming animals were on the rapid decline. Mankind's ambitions began fading as the population did as well. Global warming was no longer a nightmare, it was an immense reality. Rapidly, geneticists and the government began trying to implement a gene enhancer in humans so that the human race could survive with the fears of the wild and without sunlight, water and food. Although the change was slime, the serum had to perfectly match the genes of the human, otherwise, a serious fate could take place...

Louis Lee Jenkinson (12)
Wyvern Academy, Eggleston View

Guns And Bombs

I was alone. There was no one in sight, the doors locked. Old, dusty doorways stood tall. Cold-stoned floors were all I could see, staring out the cold, shattered, framed windows. I wondered with fear, *Am I next?* I could hear gunshots and bombs blaring out, filling my ears. Footsteps were getting closer and closer. I wasn't ready to die. I was only young, it was not my time. All of a sudden, it went dark. Silence struck. *Bang! Boom!* I stuttered in fear. All I felt was freezing, cobbled walls. I was alone once again. *Bang!*

Caitlan Morrison (11)
Wyvern Academy, Eggleston View

Extinction

It was here, the extinction. Most living creatures were wiped off the face of the Earth. It had become a war zone.

I had been living in an abandoned truck for the last few weeks, scavenging food. Every now and again, I spotted another person meandering along the deserted wastelands, seeking what they desired. It all started when our country was testing unstable nuclear weapons and they failed to successfully launch one. Now, all the air is filled with is dust that chokes you every time you inhale. Now, it's just survival of the fittest...

Thomas Klein (12)
Wyvern Academy, Eggleston View

The Beginning Of The End

The once life-filled planet has come to dust. The screams of the dead surround it but I'm not being metaphorical, the dead have risen and taken over the planet. I'm the only one left, everyone else is gone.

It all started just five days ago when they experimented on them, when they experimented on the bodies and changed them. They came down and took the dead. When they returned them they were different. They were alive again. I had to battle and hide to survive from the rest of the world. It's all their fault. It's all their fault!

Brandon Nicholson (11)
Wyvern Academy, Eggleston View

Man Vs Machine

It was dark, too dark. Wind crept through the small gap in the rusty vault door. People struggled to stay quiet as huge metal footsteps could be heard from up above. Suddenly, a huge metal Colossus burst through the door like it was made of glass. It began unleashing its wrath on the small, innocent humans. People screamed and screamed as they quickly searched for any exit close by. I luckily found one, a small cabinet filled with supplies like food, water and every weapon. I strapped them to myself with supplies and got ready to dance with the robots.

Daniel Metcalfe (13)
Wyvern Academy, Eggleston View

Reaching

Finally, I can see the once-in-a-lifetime monochromatic rock which falls into the Earth's atmosphere every century. Hopefully, this year it lands near my house.

A few minutes went by and just as I was going to leave my window ledge, my lamp shivered and then along came an earthquake-like rumble of excitement. I looked out my window and gulped. I heard the rumble of the rock enter the atmosphere, it was coming straight to me. Within seconds, it'd crashed into the middle of my street. I reached into it and something reached back...

Jack Gibson (13)
Wyvern Academy, Eggleston View

The Beginning

"Follow me," it whispered, a soldier made for war. Ruthless, relentless and the end of the world. It could run at seventy mph, hurl a car without effort and most of all, it could kill you within a second. Civilians ran like mice when spotted. All the emergency services were offline. All we had was our army who didn't stand a chance against them. It was like an ant and a boot, they have no quarrel but nothing prevents it from being squished. A light emitted from the sky. It was a flare. Little did they know, help wasn't arriving...

Arman Ahmed (13)
Wyvern Academy, Eggleston View

The Whisper

As I got down on my knees in agony, screeching, the voice began to talk in a whisper. The lights flickered! My mind was full of darkness, my life was on the line. I ran outside to the night blanket falling above the haunted town. More blood-curdling screams fell silent. It told me, "You can't run from us..." *Us?* Running as fast as I could, I finally reached my destination. The cliff! Just one more step and that was the end. I looked around to find dead bodies surrounding me like a swarm of bees. This was the end. Goodbye...

Paige McMichael (12)
Wyvern Academy, Eggleston View

Alone

"Wait!" shouted the small girl as she ran towards the departing ship. One of the workers saw the girl and held a hand out, ready to pull her on. In a burst of adrenaline, she ran faster than ever before to catch up. Though she was fast, she was still careful, checking the floor every few seconds. She got closer, close enough to almost touch the hand. In the excitement, the girl didn't notice the large rock in her way. She tripped. In the short amount of time it happened, the ship took off, leaving her alone in the apocalypse.

Aimee Eloise Bruce (13)

Wyvern Academy, Eggleston View

The Inevitable

The year 9379, the human race has now colonised every planet that isn't a gas giant. From Mercury to the dwarf Pluto. However, the greedy rulers of Mercury pushed the boundaries too far. They managed to alter the course of their planet and plunged it into the sun's fiery depths. Due to this chaos, the sun has now begun to improve. Day by day, it worsens, the sun has now begun shifting off its axis and has now begun to scorch the Earth's surface. Each day, Earth comes closer to being engulfed by the immense weight of the dying star.

Jorge Martin (14)
Wyvern Academy, Eggleston View

What Did I See?

I was lying there alone in the cold, sharp grass. It stood tall like the hair on my pale, fragile arms. I noticed the sounds of the high-pitched chirping coming from miniature birds. The sounds of ebony-brown branches snapping as birds perched themselves on the wavy green trees. It grew silent. A breeze of cold wind hit me like a bullet to my skin. Around me went dark, it was still and silent. My mind went blank and my vulnerable, shaking body shot up in astonishment. That's when I heard a helpless cry and that's when I saw it...

Courtney Spencer (13)
Wyvern Academy, Eggleston View

Then There Was One

There was that one gang. One gang that thought they were everything. Selfish, they were. The troubled trio had always wanted the whole world to know about them. I never thought they would go that far though. No one did. Roaming the streets, if they came across anyone, there would be a gun put to their head and fired. To make sure everyone was dead all over the world they decided to put bombs everywhere. A little girl that they hadn't seen, alive. She didn't know what was going on but she hated it. Gun in her hand. Silence. Death.

Holly Bainbridge (12)
Wyvern Academy, Eggleston View

Sun Explosive

It happened just when we least expected it. We knew it would happen. We knew it was this week, but not now. I was sat there, thinking, my thoughts rushing around my head. I ran up into my room, grabbed some paper and started doing my homework. It happened then. The lights went out. The windows smashed. The walls started falling down. Animals started plummeting to their deaths. I knew if I was to survive, I'd have to venture outside. I grabbed my backpack and ran outside. Then I realised it was the survival games. The sun exploded.

Katie Elizabeth Daniels (12)
Wyvern Academy, Eggleston View

The Clown Of The Lost

He used the key to unlock the door. To his horror, he saw... a maze that was called, *Clown Of The Lost.* He continued towards the entrance and a solid metal door slammed behind him. There was a scream and a clown's loud, high-pitched laugh soon followed. He raced up to where the noise came from. It was horrible. Blood dripped onto the floor, making him sick. He wiped away the remaining chunks from his mouth and flicked it away. There the noise was again, this time, the source was in sight. He could only run for his life...

Daniel Dent (13)

Wyvern Academy, Eggleston View

War End Chaos

The smoke had cleared. We weren't prepared. The machines marched and the war had begun. We sprinted towards the bunker to get our gear. We had a fair amount of experience and believed we were ready. Gunshots here, gunshots there, there was a lot going on, it was too much to handle. Buildings crashed down, people shot dead. Then the leader stepped up. You could feel the footsteps crashing, making the ground shake, making us topple. The fight seemed to be up to us to finish. This war was dreadful chaos, this was the end of chaos.

Kallumn Cooley (12)
Wyvern Academy, Eggleston View

Death Valley

I was on vacation when I heard a few gunshots. I wasn't bothered as I needed milk for my tea. I stepped out and there was a deceased corpse lying on my car. I was devastated. I ran back into my hotel, mortified by what I'd seen. I grabbed my phone, my body shivering as I called everyone in my contacts. No one answered. There was a pale, grey-skinned man whistling. I headed towards him. He stopped and looked at me. The vicious cannibal growled and sprinted after me. I hid under the chair and his footsteps went past slowly.

Ahmed Raheem Ali (13)
Wyvern Academy, Eggleston View

The Beginning Of The End

Boom. Boom. Boom. My heart was a drum, beating louder than words could describe, uncontrollable. *Boom. Boom. Boom.* Again and again, over and over. Fear crept slowly down every inch of my skin and every bone in my body, paralysing me within time. My agonising thoughts spiralled violently throughout my head, dragging me deeper and deeper into the maze that I was trapped in, stuck. No end, no way out. Hours, minutes, seconds passed, no changes, no difference, nothing. My mind was a maze, there was no way out.

Jessica Sawyer (11)
Wyvern Academy, Eggleston View

Mission Chaos

As a terrible wind flew over the once sunshine-filled beach, a large plane crashed into the pier. It had been shot down by a huge plane in a fleet of jets. All of a sudden, the group of boys who had previously been chilling on the beach all day, stood up and ran from the fleet. The massive planes opened up and aliens came out and placed flags upon the golden, sandy beach.

"The town and beach with Earth are ours!" spoke the alien king.

The boys stared at each other and were scared. Earth was doomed...

Thomas Reese (13)

Wyvern Academy, Eggleston View

Chaos

It was my favourite time of year, Halloween. I was different. People loved Christmas but I didn't. I liked it a bit but Halloween was absolutely amazing to me. The scary decorations and seeing what costumes everyone decided to wear, all the candy. Normally, when I saw someone dressed up as a murderer, I went up to them and said how great they looked. I never thought that one of these people would be a real murderer with blood all over his hands. Why me? I used to love Halloween but now I can't bear the thought.

Ellie-May Riley Caygill (12)
Wyvern Academy, Eggleston View

Is Anyone There?

Walking down the cold, dark corridor, there was a door. An old, rusty door. As I started to walk towards the door, I heard screaming coming from the corridor next to me. Lights were flickering, the door was squeaking and the scream got louder. Slowly dragging my feet across the broken floor, I went to reach out for the handle. As soon as I turned it, some weird figure moved from the corner of my eye. *What was it? Who is it?* When I turned around, I saw something I didn't want to see. I knew this was it!

Hollie Wright (13)
Wyvern Academy, Eggleston View

The Curse Of Patrick!

I was walking to my apartment one night and I had just sat down, sinking into my comfy corner couch when I noticed a dark figure in the corner of my room. I thought it could be my roommate, Adam, so I shouted, "Adam, is that you?" He slowly turned around to reveal pink-like skin, fingerless hands and bright green shorts. I reached for the phone to call 999 but it was gone. It was in his hand. Slowly, he put it up to his head and shouted, "No! This is Patrick!" and charged forwards...

Ryan Walton (14)

Wyvern Academy, Eggleston View

Don't Click Those Spam Pop-Ups!

It was a normal day, I'd searched the Web on my computer and a pop-up caught my eye. It was neon and told me I'd won the lottery. I clicked on it and downloaded the mandatory winner's programme. I opened it and suddenly I felt strange. I felt as if I just wanted to kill. Nothing could satisfy me more than fresh blood. I was dazed and confused. I wanted to just kill. I was a murder machine. It took over and I felt like vomiting. I wanted to scream, cry and punch a wall. I *wanted* to kill.

Toni Leigh Palmer (13)
Wyvern Academy, Eggleston View

Beast Strike Out

There we were, surrounded, in the middle of an airstrike field with nothing to defend us. All around, in our sight, were beasts. Terrible beasts that wanted to rip off your arms and legs to then leave you stranded. Left to die. They were running for us, there was no escape. Explosions were going off. It was a strikeout. We only had fists to help us last for a short amount of time, until help came. But, there was no help. They were coming closer. Gaps were forming in the wall of beasts, our only hope...

Jamie Day (12)
Wyvern Academy, Eggleston View

War Chaos

All I can do is bite my nails and hope for the best. We've got no power, I can't see anything and half the world is destroyed and we have no way to live. We will all be dead and there will be no humans ever again. I am in the bunker, scared whenever a bomb goes off. Everyone is in a battle to get to a car, a bunker or anywhere where they can hide and be safe. This is all wrong. The sun is dead and there is no water or food. I wish it would stop.

Matthew Dunn (12)
Wyvern Academy, Eggleston View

The Attempted Revolution

Famine drove many into prison. They needed to steal, they needed to steal to survive. Then the hunger spread and grew, taking many lives. War broke out, setting countries aflame as nuclear devices became normal, intoxicating cities. Driving them into the ground. In the colosseum like warfare, the United Kingdom came out on top but a revolution was coming. England prepped the coasts by building walls, towers and adding anti-air turrets.

Jacob Stanford (12)
Wyvern Academy, Eggleston View

How Far Can The Trends Go?

It has been days since it started. It's been hell. From what I've seen, there isn't much life anymore. No happiness, no colour. My whole family is gone. This whole thing has gone way too far. I need to put a stop to this... But how? I have no more stamina left in me to fight but I have to try. I can't let my guard down. If I can't do it, it could be the end...

Katie Louise Dixon (13)
Wyvern Academy, Eggleston View

The Abduction

All I could see was a UFO standing in front of me. It was hovering about ten feet above the air. It had white LED lights surrounding the bottom of the ship. The steamy door unveiled and in its presence was a strange-looking hat with an obscure mount of legs on it. It moved towards me, smacking its lips. The weird alien stepped towards me. I had nowhere to go...

Krish Kumar (13)
Wyvern Academy, Eggleston View

YOUNG WRITERS INFORMATION

We hope you have enjoyed reading this book – and that you will continue to in the coming years.

If you're a young writer who enjoys reading and creative writing, or the parent of an enthusiastic poet or story writer, do visit our website **www.youngwriters.co.uk**. Here you will find free competitions, workshops and games, as well as recommended reads, a poetry glossary and our blog.

If you would like to order further copies of this book, or any of our other titles, then please give us a call or order via your online account.

Young Writers
Remus House
Coltsfoot Drive
Peterborough
PE2 9BF
(01733) 890066
info@youngwriters.co.uk

Join in the conversation!

 YoungWritersUK

 @YoungWritersCW